CHANTEL NUNN

Whispers Of Vengeance

For the ones who broke,
and then built themselves into something sharper.
You are not ruined.
You are rewritten.

Acknowledgments

This is a **dark romance novel** intended for mature audiences (18+).

It contains **graphic and potentially distressing content** that may be triggering for some readers.

This story explores **dark psychological territory**, including survival, power reclamation, and the blurred lines between pleasure and pain.

While the characters find healing and love

This is not *a soft story.*

Please prioritise your well-being while reading.

You are never weak for protecting your peace.

For a full list of triggers please head to my website: https://0v4k1m-7g.myshopify.com/pages/triggers

One

Chapter 1

The last time Amelia Monroe saw him, her screams were the only sound in the room. Now, silence wrapped around her like a noose, tight and cruel. The courthouse stood ahead, tall and cold. Like a tribute to a justice system, that often forgets the ones it was supposed to protect. She hovered at the bottom of its steps, shoulders stiff and her fingers tucked deep into her coat sleeves.

Today, she had to see him again. Ethan Walker. The man who once whispered promises against her skin. The man who stole her world and claimed it as his own. The man who made safety a lie. He'd called it devotion, but it was control.

She inhaled, her breath fogging in the morning chill. You are not that girl anymore. You survived.

A hand found her back. It was warm and steady.

Lucas.

His presence was an anchor in the storm. She leaned into it, eyes fixed on the looming entrance.

"You ready?" he asked, voice low.

She turned slightly to meet his gaze. Lucas had been her constant. Yet even he was wound so tight he could break.

"No," she whispered. "But I have to do this."

He hated she had to stand before Ethan like a trophy in a courtroom of spectators. But he nodded and let his hand fall.

"I'm right beside you."

The courthouse doors parted like a wound reopening. Cameras flashed, each one a trigger. Each one a trespass.

"Ms. Monroe! Do you think the court will convict Ethan Walker?"

"Do you fear he'll walk free?"

Lucas shifted in front of her, shielding her from reporters. One glare and the questions stopped, but her heart was already racing.

Inside, the noise dissolved into a deeper silence: one of expectation. Of scrutiny and of doubt.

And then she saw him.

Ethan.

Sitting at the defence table, he looked like he belonged there. Clean-shaven. Tailored suit. Comfortable.

His posture was casual. One arm draped across the table, fingers tapping a rhythm she remembered all too well. The one he used to trace across her thigh right before the bruises bloomed.

But it was his eyes that cut through her. Cold and fixed on her as if daring her to flinch.

He tilted his head slightly. His mouth twitched. Not a smile. A secret.

Her stomach flipped. She told herself she was ready, but the moment their eyes met, her body remembered everything.

Her breath snagged. Her muscles locked, and her vision tunnelled. Because Ethan still lived inside her skin.

The judge entered, and the room hushed.

"This court is now in session for the trial of Ethan Walker, charged with kidnapping, assault and attempted murder."

Her heart thundered.

The trial had begun, and her fight for justice was on.

The charges echoed through the courtroom. Each one reopening a wound she had tried to sew shut.

Beside her, Lucas was steel, but she could feel the heat of his fury.

Ethan across the room just smirked.

The prosecutor stood. "This is not about misunderstandings. This is about violence. About control disguised as affection.About cruelty masked as love."

He turned to her. "Ms Amelia Monroe endured captivity, brutality and psychological torment. She survived the worst of someone she once trusted."

Her hands trembled. Memory clawed at her: the chains, the dark. Ethan's voice dripping lies into her ear.

Lucas brushed her hand grounding her.

She exhaled

Then the defence stood.

"Your Honour, the prosecution spins a dramatic tale. But this is not a crime. It's a lover's revenge. Ms Monroe was never held against her will. She is a woman scorned, not a victim."

Her blood ran cold.

The courtroom buzzed with whispers. Doubt bloomed.

Ethan watched her, something cruel glinting in his eyes. He knew exactly what this performance would do.

She swallowed. She'd prepared for this. But nothing could numb how it felt.

The judge nodded. "Prosecution, call your first witness."

"Ms. Monroe, please take the stand."

Lucas's touch lingered. Like letting go was wrong.

He should've protected her. He should've stopped this.

But she was already walking, shoulders square and her hands trembling.

She sat and faced the courtroom. Faced him.

"Ms Monroe," the prosecutor began. "Can you describe the night Ethan Walker took you?"

A tremor slid up her spine.

She breathed in, looked at Ethan and then began.

"It was late. Lucas and I were driving home from the Gala. Then a black SUV came out of no where and rammed us. We spun off the road and crashed."

"And what happened next?"

"I got out. Lucas did to and then they came for us."

"They?"

"Ethan's men."

A gasp rippled through the courtroom.

"We ran, into the woods. It was dark. Lucas pulled me and told me not to stop."

"And did you?"

"Yes and they caught up to us."

"They beat him. Over and over." Her voice cracked. "I screamed. They didn't stop."

Lucas sat frozen and white- knuckled.

"Ethan dragged me back to the road. Threw me in a van."

"What did he say to you?"

She met Ethan's gaze.

"You're mine again," she said.

The room recoiled.

Lucas inhaled sharply.

Ethan shifted in his seat.

"Did you go with him willingly?"

"No."

The prosecutor nodded. "No further questions."

Then came the defence.

"You once loved Ethan Walker didn't you?"

A trap.

"I did," she said. "But not the man who sits here today."

"You had a complicated relationship. Perhaps this is all just an emotional reaction."

Amelia held firm. "You're twisting what happened."

"Could it be Ethan was trying to talk to you? You panicked?"

"He bashed Lucas's skull. That's not a conversation."

"Things escalate. Maybe it just got out of hand?"

"You're asking if kidnapping got out of hand?"

The jury stirred, some shifting in their seats, others glancing toward her with new uncertainty in their eyes.

"Then why didn't he kill you?" The defence pushed. "If he's the monster you claim?"

"He didn't want me dead." Amelia said, her voice sharp and steady. " He wanted to own me."

The words hung in the air like smoke after a gunshot. Silent but suffocating. A pulse of discomfort rippled through the room. Someone coughed. A woman in the gallery looked away.

Amelia's throat burned. Her ribs felt too tight to hold the weight of her breath. She could still feel the cold of that room, the metal bite of the chains. His voice rasping against her ear like rusted wire. She wanted to claw the memory out of her skin.

Across the aisle, Ethan's smirk finally faded. Just for a moment.

The judge's gavel cracked once and then again. "Order in the court."

The defence attorney blinked. Her grip on her folder tightened.

"No further questions."She said her voice thinner now.

Amelia stood and walked back to Lucas.

Across the room Ethan watched.

This wasn't the end. But she could feel it coming. And when it did, she'd be the one holding the knife.

Two

Chapter 2

The television flickered in Ethan's cell, its blue light crawling over the cinder blocks like water over a grave.

CNN: again.

He liked this reporter. Calm, polished, mouth carved into a sympathetic smile, sharp enough to gut someone without them noticing.

"…as the jury deliberates the remaining charges, questions have emerged around Amelia Monroe's emotional reliability. Her previous romantic involvement with the accused has blurred the line between trauma and consent…."

Ethan smiled.

They were starting to understand. Finally.

The nuance. The grey. The art of blurred memory and rewritten truth.

That's what he'd always told Amelia. "No one will ever see

it the way we do, baby but that's what makes it real."

He reclined against the cold wall, one arm loose in his lap, the other cradling his head like a man enjoying the quiet before a storm.

She was beautiful on screen. Even through pixelation. Chin lifted, lips tight and shoulders pulled like wire. That hollow stare in her eyes. He knew it intimately. He'd carved it there, layer by layer.

It made her *real* and it made her *his*.

A guard passed by, paused long enough to glance at the screen. Ethan didn't blink.

"Looks like she's getting brave," the guard muttered.

Ethan's smile stretched slow. Patient. Poisonous. "She always was."

"She'll bury you before this is over," the guard scoffed.

Ethan turned his head lazily, eyes glinting something cold behind the calm.

"She's not trying to bury me," he said. "She's trying to crawl out of me."

The guard stiffened. Keys jingled like warning bells at his hip.

"She looked pretty done with you to me."

Ethan's gaze snapped to him. Slow and deliberate. Not angry, just observant. Like a scientist watching a rat twitch in a trap it set for itself.

"She said that once before," he murmured. "Right after I broke her voice box screaming."

The guard flinched.

Ethan's voice softened to something almost reverent. "But the silence afterward? That was worship. That was understanding."

The television's glow danced over his face, shadows stretching across his bruised eyes like a crown. He didn't look unhinged. He looked *holy.*

The guard stepped back. It was just a fraction but Ethan noticed.

He always noticed.

"You afraid of me?" he asked, voice barely audible. "You should be. Not because I'll hurt you, that's easy."

He leaned forward, elbows to knees and shadows clinging to his frame like smoke.

"No. You should be afraid because men like me don't die in a cage. We wait. We rot. We learn the names of your children. We map your habits. And then, when the world forgets…"

He snapped his fingers, soft and slow. "…we remind them."

The guard didn't speak again. Just walked away, too fast, shoulders tense.

Ethan reclined back, calm as the dead.

The screen shifted. A new still photo of Amelia. Her mouth parted mid- testimony, jaw tight and eyes brimming with defiance.

He'd taught her that.

"She'll come back," he whispered." They always do."

And his mind drifted into a memory.

But not how it happened. How *he* remembered it.

Their room. Not the one with the bloodstains and chains but the one behind his eyelids. Clean. Warm. Hers.

She wore white. Not the shredded dress from the night he dragged her screaming into the van but something purer.

She looked at him with fire but *longing.*

"Ethan," she whispered. Trembling. Grateful. "You found me."

He cupped her face so gently. The same hands that bruised her ribs now traced her cheek like scripture.

"I told you I would," he whispered. "No one sees you the way I do."

And she smiled. Lips split from begging but curved upward like she finally understood.

"Please," she'd murmured, fingertips curled against his chest. "Don't let them take me back."

He obliged. He always gave her what she truly needed.

The rest blurred. Sensation and heat, pain reframed as passion. She whimpered beneath him not in protest, but in melody. Her nails raked his skin not to escape but to *hold*. The blood between them? Sacred.

She kissed him. He was sure of it. Right before he whispered *mine* into her mouth.

Right before she shattered around him.

And when she lay there trembling, he didn't see terror.

He saw surrender, because it was never the bruises.

Never the screams. It was the silence, the beautiful obedient silence.

Ethan's eyes opened slowly.

The television buzzed on, forgotten. The world thought him caged.

But cages were for bodies, not minds.

He still had a voice and he knew where to whisper it.

The courthouse intern. Shy little thing with shaky hands. She'd smiled at him once. One letter later, unsigned, elegantly penned.

Chapter 2

You don't know who she is. Look deeper. Ask the nurse at Midtown General. She lied once. She'll do it again.

-E

A podcast host, addicted to cases involving blurred consent, received a flash drive. Grainy clips of Amelia's voice saying "I love you," sliced from context. Her laughter. The click of a belt. A sigh.

All voluntary. All seductive. All a lie. But lies told often enough become truths in the right ears.

A community college professor, morally flexible and obsessed with redemption arc, began reading his letters aloud during lectures. Philosophy wrapped in barbed wire.

He smiled. His roots were spreading in soil Amelia couldn't see. And the rot would bloom.

The forums were easy. Ghost accounts, breadcrumb trails, conspiracy whispers.

Didn't Amelia keep going back to him? Strange how quickly she fell for the next man. Don't victims usually avoid sex?

He knew the world. Knew how to weaponize doubt. They didn't have to believe him completely. They just had to question *her*.

Ethan leaned back, hands folded behind his head.

"She thinks the trial is the end," he murmured. "But it's just the beginning."

The guard passed again, eyes flickering to the faint graffiti Ethan had scratched into the wall, an elaborate spiral surrounded by names only *he* understood.

He didn't look up.

But the guard walked faster this time.

She'll never be free.

Not until she learns that freedom is whatever *he* decides to give her.

Three

Chapter 3

It smelled like forgotten justice with stale coffee, worn leather, and the ghosts of a hundred bad verdicts. Each breath Amelia took scraped against her lungs like glass. The jury had been out for hours, but it felt like days. Each passing minute another cruel stretch of uncertainty that gnawed at her sanity.

She sat rigid, hands clenched so tight in her lap her knuckles burned white, and her nails digging crescents into her skin. The polished bench beneath her was cold, biting into her bones.

Voices murmured behind her, feet shuffled, and she felt the weight of every single gaze piercing her back like a hundred tiny blades. Beside her, Lucas was still and silent. His shoulders wound tight with fury and dread. His hand rested on his thigh so close to hers she could feel the heat radiating off him. But he hadn't touched her. Not here in front of the world.

God, she wished he would, though. She wished she could

lean into him, let his presence wrap around her. Let his darkness shield her from the eyes watching. But she forced her spine straight, chin high and refused to let Ethan see even the slightest fracture in her armour. Because he was watching. She didn't need to look to know. His gaze seared through her like a phantom touch that dragged across her skin and left her trembling. Even now, free of his chains, she could still feel him reaching for her from across the room.

The Bailiff's voice cut through her haze. "All rise."

Chairs scraped against the floor. Amelia's knees wobbled but she locked them tight. Her body vibrating with the effort to remain upright.

The jurors filed in, their expressions carved from stone, and their eyes avoiding hers.

Each beat of silence slammed into her chest like a hammer.

The judge's voice rang out. "Has the jury reached a verdict?"

A woman rose, the paper trembling in her hand. "We have, Your Honour."

"Please read the verdict."

The woman unfolded the paper with a rustle that roared in Amelia's ears louder than any scream.

"In the case of Ethan Walker versus the State, on the charge of kidnapping, we find the defendant...."

The pause stretched for what felt like an eternity.

"Not guilty."

The words tore through her like a blade.

Not guilty.

For a moment, the world tilted. Her knees threatened to buckle, but she locked them, her breath coming in ragged and broken bursts. Her vision narrowed to the smirk curling

Ethan's lips. Slow and deliberate, spreading across his face like rot.

He was winning.

He always won.

A ripple of disbelief shivered through the courtroom. The sharp crack of a phone hitting the ground echoed like a warning shot, dragging Amelia out of the fog of her past.

Her gaze followed to a woman in the second row. Dark hair pulled into a low bun. Her eyes met Amelia's from across the room. There was rage and heartbreak behind them but also something else. Something deeper.

Belief.

The woman pressed her hand over her mouth trying to fight tears and gave the slightest no. A silent promise:

I see you. I believe you.

Amelia's chest tightened. Tears burned behind her eyes. That single nod anchored her to the earth for a fleeting moment. That was until Ethan smiled and the fragile thread of hope shattered beneath his gaze.

Her stomach twisted violently. Bile scorched her throat. The judge's voice blurred around her as he addressed the jury again.

"And on the charge of attempted murder?"

The woman's voice steadied as she read. "We find the defendant….guilty."

The room exploded in noise. The gavel slammed down, the judge roaring for order but Amelia barely heard him. Her gaze stayed locked on Ethan.

He didn't move. Didn't even flinch. That damned smirk stayed glued to his face.

The judge's voice cut through the chaos. "Mr Walker, you

have been found guilty of attempted murder. Sentencing will take place in two weeks. Until then you will remain in custody."

Two weeks. Two weeks until he learned his fate. Two weeks for him to twist and manipulate, to find cracks in the system and slip through them like the monster he was.

It wasn't enough but at least it was something.

The bailiffs approached him, cuffs in hand. Ethan didn't resist. Didn't even blink. And as they led him past her, his gaze found hers. Amelia's breath stalled in her chest.

He winked. A single wink triggered her body into a violent memory.

Cold tile under her spine. The flickering hum of the basement light. The sharp metallic tang of blood on her tongue. His breath on her cheek. Hot and suffocating.

Her vision blurred, vertigo sweeping through her body as the courtroom spun. Then he was gone.

A sob wrenched from her chest. Her knees buckled.

Lucas caught her before she hit the floor.

"I've got you," he whispered into her ear. He cradled her against his chest, shielding her trembling body with his own. Cameras clicked. Gasps echoed through the gallery, but he didn't care.

He carried her out, his arms iron around her. Her tears hot against his neck.

The SUV was silent except for the patter of rain against the windows. Streetlights smeared past in a haze of colour that she couldn't process.

"Not guilty for kidnapping," she whispered, her voice like a ghost in the dark.

Lucas's hands clenched around the steering wheel, his jaw ticking with rage.

"Bullshit."

She turned. "They never saw the van. No cameras. No evidence. Just my word."

"Your word should have been enough."

"It never is," she whispered.

Silence stretched heavy between them. Lucas pulled into his underground car park and cut the engine. "You're not going home."

"Lucas…"

"No." His voice sharp and final. "You're staying with me."

A chill crawled up her spine. He was right. Ethan wasn't done. She could feel it in her bones.

"Okay." She whispered.

He exhaled, relief flickering across his face before he reached over brushing his fingers lightly over her wrist. "Come inside."

The elevator doors closed behind them and in that moment her body shuddered. Her arms wrapping around herself while her mind spiralled into darkness.

Lucas cursed softly and pulled her into his arms. One hand cradled the back of her head while the other pressed firmly against her spine. Anchoring her trembling body to his.

"I've got you," he murmured into her hair. His lips brushed her temple.

She clung to him, fingers twisting into his shirt. For the first time since the trial began she let herself collapse.

Lucas pulled back just enough to cup her face, tilting her chin up to meet his gaze.

"Amelia…."His voice cracked softly.

Her breath hitched. For the first time in a long time, she wasn't afraid to feel. Not with him.

And then her phone buzzed. Her stomach dropped, the phone suddenly too heavy in her hand.

Unknown Number:

Did you really think this was over?

Four

Chapter 4

The house was too quiet.

Amelia sat curled into the far corner of the couch, knees drawn to her chest beneath the blanket wrapped tight around her. The flickering television cast a glow across her face. From the kitchen doorway, Lucas watched her, his chest aching with helplessness. He held a mug of tea between his hands. Her favourite was jasmine and honey, at least had been before everything shattered.

He didn't know if it still was. He didn't know what parts of her remained untouched by him, by Ethan, and by the darkness that swallowed their lives whole.

Crossing the room quietly, he placed the mug on the table beside her. She didn't move. Didn't blink. Didn't flinch.

"I added honey," he said softly.

Her fingers twitched around the blanket. "Thanks."

He sat down on the opposite end of the couch. Not too close

to crowd her, but close enough to remind her he was there; that he wasn't leaving.

"Have you eaten today?" he asked, his eyes tracing the shadows beneath hers.

She shook her head once. "Not hungry."

Lucas leaned forward, elbows on his knees. "Talk to me, Amelia."

For a long moment, she didn't move. Then her gaze flickered to his, and she saw something dark and distant.

"There's nothing to say," she whispered, her voice flat and empty. "It's over."

He shook his head slowly. "No. It's not. Not for you."

Silence stretched between them. Then her eyes lifted to his again and for the first time that day, he saw her break. Saw the raw, unguarded wound behind her numbness.

"Do you still want me?" she asked.

Her words weren't seductive. They were broken glass in her throat, bleeding out all the fear she couldn't swallow.

Lucas's chest tightened. His reply came out hoarse, stripped bare. "I never stopped."

She blinked, tears glistening but refusing to fall. "I can't feel anything. Not really. It's like…I'm here, but I'm not."

"I know," he murmured. "You don't have to pretend with me."

"I want to pretend it never happened. That I'm still the woman who smiled when you looked at me."

He shifted closer. "You're still her, Amelia. She's just hiding right now. And I'll wait as long as it takes for her to come back."

A shuddered breath left her lips. She reached for the mug,

cradling it between her hands like an anchor but didn't drink.

"I'm scared I won't come back," she whispered. "That I'll stay numb forever."

Lucas closed his eyes, forcing down the ache in his chest. When he spoke, his voice trembled with truth. "I'm scared too. Not of you breaking. Of pushing too hard. Of hurting you when all I want is to hold you together."

She blinked rapidly, tears slipping free. "You're not the one who hurts me."

"Then let me help."

Her fingers tightened around the mug. "I don't know how."

He reached out, then slow and careful, brushing a strand of hair from her face and tucking it gently behind her ear.

"Start with this," he murmured. "Let me hold you."

She hesitated for a moment then with a tiny nod, she placed the mug onto the table.

Lucas opened his arms and she crawled into them, her body trembling with the force of everything she had locked away.

He gathered her in gently, wrapping his arms around her like she was made of glass and steel all at once.

Minutes passed. Maybe hours. The world outside moved on but inside that room time stilled.

Eventually her shaking eased. Her breath soft and slow against his neck.

Then, so quiet it was almost lost in the hush around them, she spoke.

"When you touched me before… when we…. when you took control… I felt safe."

Lucas's breath stalled in his chest.

"But now…" Her voice cracked, trembling. "I'm scared I'll ruin that. That I'll freeze or panic and ruin you."

He pulled back just enough to look into her eyes, his hands cupping her face with aching tenderness. "You couldn't ruin me, Amelia," he whispered. "But we don't go back to that unless *you* want it. Crave it. Choose it. Not because you think I need it."

Tears spilled down her cheeks. She shook her head weakly. "What if I want it again? What if I need it to remember who I am?"

"Then we take it slow. And if you say yes and halfway through you can't...."

"Even if I freeze?"

"Especially then," he said, his voice fierce and gentle all at once. "We stop. No questions. No guilt."

She let out a broken sob, burying her face into his chest. "Okay," she breathed. "Not now. But ....soon, maybe."

Lucas pressed his lips to her forehead, lingering there like a silent promise.

"I'll wait," he whispered into her hair.

Lucas held her carefully. Her tears soaked into his shirt, searing straight through to his chest, leaving an ache he couldn't name.

He pressed his lips to her hair, breathing her in. Jasmine shampoo. Salt tears. The faintest trace of fear. He wanted to erase it all. Replace it with safety. With himself.

But he didn't know how.

God, he thought, tightening his hold just slightly. *How do I fix this?*

He'd built empires. Torn down men twice his size with a single look. Broken people with his words alone. But here, holding her, he felt powerless. Useless. Like nothing he had ever learned in his cutthroat world mattered.

All he wanted was to keep her safe. To see her smile again. Not the brittle, haunted twist of her lips she forced for others, but her real smile. The one that lit her eyes with mischief and warmth. The one that made him feel like there was still something good in him, something worth her touch.

He swallowed hard, his throat tight with grief and rage. Rage at Ethan for what he'd done, for the way he'd stolen her light and twisted it into something broken. For the way he hadn't been able to protect her before. Grief for the girl she'd been before him. The girl Lucas would never know. The girl he could only catch glimpses of in fleeting moments when her guard cracked.

He brushed his thumb over her temple, feeling the fine tremor still vibrating through her. *I would burn the world to the ground for you,* he thought. *I would rip out his throat with my bare hands if it meant you could sleep without fear.*

She shifted slightly, her fingers still curled into his shirt like a lifeline. He felt her begin to drift, exhaustion finally overpowering the chaos in her mind.

Lucas stayed perfectly still, cradling her against him, his own heart thudding slow and heavy beneath her ear. He knew sleep wouldn't come for him tonight. His mind was already whirring with silent and violent promises. He tilted his head back against the couch cushion, staring up at the ceiling as darkness pooled around them.

I don't care how many laws I have to break, he thought coldly. *I don't care who I have to become.*

His eyes closed, his jaw tight with resolve.

I will make sure he never touches you again. Even if I have to become a monster to do it.

He tightened his hold on her, feeling her breathing even out as sleep claimed her.

Chapter 5

The hotel room was bathed in amber light, jazz playing from an old speaker. The bed was king-sized, sheets crisp and white. The smell of wine and cologne clinging to the air like something rotten beneath the sweetness.

Amelia sat cross-legged at the edge of the mattress, flushed from alcohol and Ethan's kisses. She wore only one of his dress shirts, the fabric falling over her thighs like silk. Her skin tingled where his hands had been.

Ethan watched her from the armchair across the room, swirling the last inch of wine in his glass. There was a sharpness in his gaze tonight. Something hungry and mean.

"I've been thinking," he said. His voice soft but lined with steel. "You like it when I take control."

She blinked, her mind fogged by alcohol. "I mean... sometimes yeah. But we haven't really talked about...."

"I didn't ask if we had talked about it," he snapped, smile still curling his lips but his eyes had gone flat. "I said you liked it. You like not having to think. Not having to decide."

She hesitated, swallowing a lump that had formed in her throat. "I like feeling safe."

His smiled widened. He set his glass down and stood, crossing the room in two silent strides.

His hands closed around her thighs, fingers digging into soft flesh, forcing them apart. Not gently. Not lovingly. Just taking.

"Then let me make you feel that way," he murmured his breath hot against her cheek.

She nodded shakily. "…Okay…"

"Say, 'Yes, Sir'"

She let out a small nervous laugh." What?"

His grip tightened, fingertips pressing into muscle and bone. Her laugh died instantly.

"Say it,' he ordered, his voice low and dangerous. "Say 'Yes Sir,' or I'll make you wish you had."

Her heart thudded painfully against her ribs, fear spiking cold through her veins. Some part of her wanted to run. But deeper still there was that desperate little voice inside her. The one that needed his approval like oxygen.

"Yes, Sir."

His eyes darkened with satisfaction. "Good girl."

He pushed her back onto the mattress roughly, the springs creaking beneath her.

He climbed over her, pressing his weight down until her lungs felts squeezed. His hands wrapped around her wrists, pinning them above her head. He kissed her hard, teeth dragging across her bottom lip until her tasted blood.

But her didn't stop.

His hand slid up to her throat, fingers wrapping around it. Thumb pressing lightly against her pulse point. Not tight enough to cut off her air. Not yet.

"Look at you," he murmured against her mouth, his voice thick with dark satisfaction.

"You're so fucking pretty when you're scared."

Her eyes widened, panic flashing through them. She tried to pull back but his grip tightened instantly around her neck, holding her in place.

"Don't move," he ordered, his tone calm and flat. He shifted, pinning her wrists above her head with one hand while the other pressed harder into her throat. Just enough to make her chest burn with the effort of dragging in air.

Her thighs trembled beneath him. She couldn't look away from his face. The flicker of amber light casting harsh shadows across his cheekbones. There was no warmth in his eyes now. No affection. Just cold hunger. Possession.

"Please," she whispered, her voice small and choked.

"Please what?" he asked, titling his head as if genuinely curious. "Please stop? Please keep going? You don't even know, do you?'

Tears slipped from the corners of her eyes, sliding hot down her temples into her hair. She couldn't answer. All she knew was the terror crawling up her spine and the numbness in her fingers where he was pinning her wrists too tightly and the ache in her chest as her breaths came shorter and faster.

He laughed softly, darkly. "That's what I thought."

His hands slid down from her throat to her chest, fingers digging painfully into her ribs as he dragged the shirt open, buttons popping and scattering across the sheets. The fabric tore under his grip, baring her trembling body.

She flinched, instinctively trying to cover herself but his grip on her wrists didn't falter.

He leaned down, lips brushing the shell of her ear, voice dropping to a low dangerous whisper.

"Mine,"he said. "All of you. Every inch. Every breath. You gave it to me the moment you said yes."

Her pulse roared in her ears, a deafening thunder of fear and shame.

He bit her earlobe, hard enough to make her gasp in pain. His free hand roamed lower, fingers pressing into soft flesh with bruising force. She felt her body clench in panic, chest heaving with ragged breaths.

"Don't cry," he said, his tone almost gentle as he kissed the tears from her cheek, each touch burning with cold cruelty. "You'll ruin your pretty face."

But she couldn't stop. The sob broke free before she could swallow it down, her shoulders shaking as the tears fell harder. She turned her head away, pressing her face into the pillow to muffle the sounds.

For a second the room fell silent except for her ragged breaths. Then his hand shot out, fingers wrapping around her jaw and yanking her face back to him. His eyes burned with sudden rage, his nostrils flaring as his mouth twisted into something cruel and monstrous.

"I told you not to fucking cry, you stupid little slut," he snarled.

Before she could blink, his palm cracked across her cheek with a force that sent stars bursting behind her eyes. The slap echoed through the room. Sharp and violent. The sting burning deep into her bone. Her head snapped to the side, hair whipping across her face as a choked sob tore from her throat.

She tasted blood. Coppery and hot where her teeth had cut into her cheek. Pain radiated out in sickening waves, her vision blurring with tears and dizziness. She tried to move way, her body instinctively curling inward but his hand fisted in her hair, yanking her head back so hard her neck screamed with pain.

"You think you can fucking ignore me?" he spat his breath hot against her face, smelling of wine and anger. "You think you get to decide when to cry? When to speak? When to fucking breath?"

She whimpered, tears streaming down her burning cheek. "I...I'm sorry," she gasped, her voice breaking. " P...please, Ethan."

"Please what?" he sneered, his grip tightening until her scalp burned. "Please stop? Please forgive you? You're nothing without me. You hear me? Nothing."

His other hand grabbed her throat, squeezing just enough to choke off her breath. Her chest heaving in silent panic. Her pulse thundered in her ears, vision narrowing to his face twisted with fury above her.

"You're mine," he growled. "Every fucking inch of you belongs to me. And if you ever fucking cry without my permission again."

He squeezed harder, cutting of her air completely. One, two, three until blackness crept in at the edges of her vision and her body convulsed in terror.

Then he released her throat with a shove, letting her collapse onto the mattress, gasping and coughing. Tears and saliva dripping down her chin as she scrambled to pull air into her lungs.

He watched her with disgust, wiping his hands on the bed sheet as if her skin had tainted him.

"Pathetic," he murmured, his voice flat and cold. "Clean yourself up."

She didn't move at first, her body trembling too hard to obey. He reached out suddenly, grabbing her hair again and dragging her head up until their eyes met.

"Did you hear me?" He snapped.

"Yes," she whispered,tears dripping from her chin onto his wrist.

He shoved her away, letting her fall back onto the bed in a heap of trembling limbs and silent sobs. For a moment, he just stood there, watching her with dark empty eyes.

Then he climbed into bed beside her, pulling the blankets up like nothing had happened. Like he hadn't just torn her apart with his hands and words.

Amelia lay frozen beneath the weight of the covers, her skin crawling with the echoes of what he'd just done.

Beside her, Ethan's breathing slowed, steady and satisfied.

She waited until the rhythm of his breath evened out until she was sure he wouldn't reach for her again.

Then, slowly and carefully she slipped from the bed.

Her bare feet hit the floor with a soft thud. Every step toward the bathroom felt like walking on egg shells. Her body stiff and aching. The bathroom light buzzed overhead. She stared at her reflection, barely recognising herself. Her eyes were hollow, mascara streaked down her cheeks like war paint. A bruise was already forming beneath her collarbone and her lips were split and swollen.

She reached for a washcloth and turned on the tap, letting the water run until it was hot.

She scrubbed until her skin was raw and pink, until she could no longer feel the phantom press of his hands or the sting of his words. But it didn't help. Not really. The filth was inside her. Under her skin and in her bones.

Tears spilled silently down her cheeks as she gripped the edge of the sink, trying to steady her breath.

You'll survive. You always do.

She didn't believe it but she whispered it to herself anyway.

When she finally turned off the water, her hands were shaking. She dried off slowly. Then crept back into the bedroom, crawling into the bed as quietly as possible.

Ethan stirred and rolled over to face her. He pressed a kiss to her hair soft and possessive.

"Good girl," he murmured, pulling her against his chest as if she were something precious.

She lay stiff and silent in his arms, her body shaking with sobs she forced back down her throat until she felt numb.

Because arguing felt dangerous.

Because moving felt dangerous.

Because *breathing* felt dangerous.

And as her drifted off to sleep, his arm heavy around her waist, only one thought pulsed through her mind...

I'm not sure I'm getting out of this alive.

Six

Chapter 6

Morning light crept through the curtains, casting fractured patterns across the wooden floor. It should have felt warm. Safe. But the air carried a heaviness that clung to her skin.

Amelia sat on the edge of the bed, freshly showered. Wrapped in one of Lucas's oversized T-shirts. Damp hair clung to her neck. She stared down at her bare feet, grounding herself in the grain of the floorboards.

She'd slept, not well though. Dreams had clawed at her all night, dragging her under and spitting her out breathless in the dark. But it had been enough to dull the sharpest edges of exhaustion. Enough to want for a moment to feel human again.

In the kitchen, Lucas moved with quiet purpose. His back to her as he flipped pancakes. The scent of cinnamon curled through the air, warm and soft.

She stepped into the kitchen, her voice low. "Smells good."

Lucas glanced over his shoulder, a small smile touching his lips. "You like cinnamon right?"

She nodded, something loosening in her chest. "Still do."

He plated up the pancakes and slid them onto the kitchen island. She climbed onto the stool, took a bite and closed her eyes. The sweetness, the spice it wasn't just good. It was grounding. The taste of a morning that could almost be normal. When she opened her eyes, Lucas was watching her with an expression so tender it made her throat ache.

"I've missed this." He said softly.

She swallowed. "What? Me eating pancakes?"

His smiled flickered sad and warm. " No. Seeing you breathe."

Amelia lowered her gaze to her plate, blinking back sudden tears. "It's hard. Like my body forgot how to be normal."

He reached across the counter, his palm open, waiting. She placed her hand in his without thinking.

"Whatever normal is for you now," he said, his thumb brushing her knuckles. "We'll find it. Together."

They ate mostly in silence but it wasn't heavy. It was a quiet that felt like safety.

Later, in the living room, Amelia stood by the window. Watching the world go on down below. Her reflection ghosted in the glass. Pale, hollowed-eyed and using Lucas's shirt like it was armour. Behind her, Lucas's footsteps approached slow and careful.

"You okay?" he asked.

She nodded then turned to face him. Her heart thudded painfully in her chest.

"I want to try something." she said, her voice barely above a whisper.

Lucas stilled. "Okay."

Her hands trembled as she reached for him. "Kiss me. Like before. Just……..just a kiss."

His eyes darkened not with lust but with something deeper. Understanding. He stepped forward, close but not overwhelming.

"If you need me to stop, say so." He murmured.

"I will."

He cupped her check, thumb brushing against her temple. He lowered his mouth to hers. The kiss was slow. Deep. Familiar. His lips tasted like cinnamon and promise.

For a fleeting moment, her body remembered safety. Her fingers curled into the hem of his shirt, clinging to him, needing more. Then it hit her. Cold tile beneath her spine. The burning metal biting into her wrists. Ethan's breath, hot and rancid in her ear.

Her chest seized. The room vanished.

She shoved him back, panic flooding her veins like ice water. "Stop."

Lucas froze instantly, his hands raised and his eyes wide with gentle alarm. "It's okay," he said softly. "You're safe. I've got you."

She shook her head, tears streaming down her cheeks. "I thought I was ready."

"You were brave to try," he murmured, voice rough with emotion. "That matters more."

Her breath came in short, trembling bursts. "I just…. I wanted to feel like myself again."

He stepped forward, slowly and carefully until she felt his warmth close again.

"Then let me help you remember who you are," he whispered. "We don't have to rush. We can just be quiet. Or I can hold you. Whatever you need."

She let out a broken sound, a half sob and half sigh. She buried her face in his chest. His arms closed around her instantly, strong and gentle. Anchoring her to the moment, to him.

They stood like that for a long time, the world outside moving on without them.

But as the sun dipped low, painting the sky in purples and fading gold, a knock shattered the quiet.

Amelia stiffened.

Lucas moved to the door, checking the peephole before opening it just wide enough to take the envelope from the courier standing there. He shut the door and turned it over in his hands, his jaw tightening.

"What is it?" Amelia asked.

He didn't answer. Just tore the seal open and pulled out a photograph.

A red circle was drawn around her on the photograph. Below it a single message:

Still mine.

Amelia stepped back, her breath snagging in her throat as the walls closed in around her. Her vision blurred as she stared at the photograph in Lucas's hands. Cold swept through her veins and her legs trembled beneath her.

"No..." she whispered. "No....no...no"

Lucas's jaw clenched so tight she could hear his teeth grind.

His eyes burned with something dark and murderous as he stared down at the photo.

She couldn't look away.

It wasn't a recent picture. It was her, naked. Chained to a bed she prayed she would never see again. Her wrists strapped down metal biting into her skin and her face streaked with tears. Her eyes were swollen, vacant and staring at something beyond the camera. Beyond him. Beyond hope.

A broken sound tore from her throat. Her knees gave out, slamming into the hardwood floor as she collapsed. Her fingers dug into her scalp, yanking her damp hair as silent screams ripped through her chest.

Lucas dropped the photo and fell to his knees in front her. "Amelia," he growled his voice trembling with fury he could barely leash. "Look at me."

She didn't hear him. Tears streamed down her cheeks, her body shaking so hard her teeth clacked together.

"He's coming for me," she sobbed rocking back and forth. "He's coming for me, Lucas. He's going to finish it. He's going to....."

"Amelia!" His voice cracked like thunder, sharp and commanding. Her wide, tear soaked eyes finally meeting his. "Listen to me. He's not getting near you. He's rotting in a cell and if he ever gets out. I will put him in the ground myself."

Her chest heaved, lungs burning with panic. "He took that...he took that when... I was there. When he....." Her voice broke into a sob. "He kept it. All this time, he kept it...."

Lucas's expression darkened. He turned and snatched the photo from the floor, ripping it clean down the middle. Then again and again until only shredded strips remained in his fists.

He threw them aside, his body vibrating with barely contained violence. Slowly he stood, his hands curling into fists at his sides.

"Stay here." he said, his voice low and murderous.

"Lucas...."

But he didn't hear her. He was already moving, grabbing his phone from the counter with shaking fingers.

"Get everyone to the penthouse now." He barked into the phone. "I want eyes on every guard in that prison. I don't give a fuck what it costs. Find out who helped him get this to her."

He paused, shoulders trembling. His head lowering as his free hand gripped the counter until his knuckles were white.

"And when you find them," he said, his voice dropping to a low lethal whisper. "You bring them to me. Alive."

He ended the call and tossed the phone aside. The silence in the room pulsed thick and heavy with his rage.

Then he turned back to Amelia.

She was still on the floor, curled in on herself. Sobbing into her knees. Her entire body trembling with fear. Her eyes met his as he approached. He dropped to his knees beside her and pulled her into his arms. She flinched at first but then collapsed against him, clutching his shirt, her tears soaking through the fabric.

"I've got you," he whispered into her hair. "I swear to God, Amelia. He's never touching you again. I'll kill every last person who helps him breathe if I have to."

Her sobs broke in his chest. "He's going to finish it..... he's going to take me back."

"No. No one is taking you anywhere." He pressed his lips to her temple.

Lucas carried her to the bathroom, her body limp in his arms. Tears still streaming down her face. He set her gently on the closed toilet lid and turned on the shower, steam beginning to fill the room.

"Come on, angel," he murmured. "Let's wash today off you."

She didn't respond. Didn't move. Her eyes were glassy, staring at nothing. Her breathing shallow and uneven.

"Amelia," he said firmer this time. Crouching in front of her. His hands cupped her face, thumbs brushing away her tears. "I need you to stand up for me."

Her gaze flickered to his. Slowly and shakily she rose. He pulled the oversized t-shirt over her head, leaving her bare in the cool air. Her skin pebbled instantly, goosebumps racing across her arms and thighs but she didn't react.

Lucas led her into the shower, stepping in behind her, still fully clothed. Warm water ran down her shoulders, flattening her hair against her neck. For a moment she just stood there motionless. Then a small sound broke from her lips. A soft choked sob that echoed off the tiled walls.

Her knees buckled. She collapsed to the floor of the shower. Water splashed around her, soaking Lucas's jeans as he knelt beside her. She pressed her forehead to her knees, her body rocking with the force of her breakdown. Her cries were raw, pulled from the deepest darkest place inside her. The place she never let anyone see.

"Amelia. It's OK. I'm here. I've got you, just let it all out." But she couldn't hear him over the screaming in her mind. Over the echo of Ethan's voice snarling *mine, mine, mine* over and over.

"I can't…" she sobbed. "I cant do this again."

Lucas grabbed her wrists gently but firmly, pulling them away from her body. He slid his arms around her, pressing her soaking and trembling body into his chest. Water poured down them both, soaking his hair and clothes. But he didn't care.

"Breathe angel." He whispered. "In and out, come one. In and out follow my breathing."

Her breaths hitched but then slowly fell into rhythm with his until her sobs turned into quiet, broken whimpers. Lucas held her tighter.

"I've got you." he whispered. "I sweat to God, Amelia. He will never touch you again. Even if I have to rip out his fucking throat myself."

Seven

Chapter 7

The candlelight flickered against rain-streaked windows, shadows dancing across Ethan's face. Amelia sat cross-legged at the edge of the bed wearing only one of his shirts, the fabric damp against her flushed skin. Outside thunder rumbled low and endless.

"You hate the rain," she murmured, tracing small circles on the bed sheet.

Ethan tilted his head, his gaze sharpening. "I used to."

She forced a small smile." What changed?"

"You."

His answer was instant, sliding into her like a blade between ribs. He stood and crossed the room. When he sat beside her, the mattress dipped under his weight causing her body to tip toward him. His scent wrapped around her; cologne, wine and something dark.

"You're the calm in it," he said, fingers drifting up her bare thigh, trailing higher until she flinched. "The eye of the storm."

She swallowed, her voice small. "That's….dramatic."

Ethan's smile curved, but there was no warmth behind it. Only teeth. "I don't do mild, Amelia. Not with you. Don't you feel it?"

She nodded, fear coiling in her gut.

The way he looked at her made her feel devoured. Like he could see every secret, she'd ever hidden and planned to take them all for himself.

"I've never wanted anyone like this," he whispered. His hand sliding under the hem of the shirt to grip her hip. His thumb pressed into the bone, hard enough to bruise. "It's dangerous how much I want you."

"Ethan….."

Suddenly his grip tightened painfully, yanking her onto her back. She gasped as her spine hit the mattress. Before she could move, he was over her. One knee pressing down on the sheets beside her ribs, one hand wrapped tight around her throat.

"Ethan….stop….."

He squeezed lightly, just enough to choke off her word. His face lowering until his mouth brushed her ear.

"You're mine," he hissed. "You're my girl, Amelia. My tight little cunt to fuck whenever I want."

She whimpered, tears pricking her eyes as fear surged cold through her veins.

He pressed his palm harder against her throat cutting off her next sob. As the other hand ripped the shirt up over her breasts.

"Look at you," he sneered, his eyes roaming her trembling

exposed body. "So fucking pretty when you're scared."

Her chest burned with trapped air. Her vision darkening at the edges. Her hands flew up to grab his wrist and nails digging into his skin with desperation.

"Don't fight," he said softly, almost gently. His thumb stroking her jaw. "Don't ever fucking fight me."

He shifted his knee sliding between her legs, forcing them apart. She sobbed, the sound ragged and broken under his grip.

"Good girl," he purred leaning down to drag his tongue up the side of her throat. "Cry for me."

His teeth sank into the soft flesh under her ear, hard enough to leave a mark that would bloom purple and black by morning.

"You hate this, don't you?" his lips brushing against hers. "But you love it too. You love being my little whore. My perfect fuck toy."

She shook her head, eyes wide with terror.

He laughed, low and cruel. "Don't lie to me."

His free hand slid between her thighs, forcing her open wider. The humiliation burned deep inside her.

"You're so fucking wet for me," he said his voice dark with satisfaction. "My good girl. Always ready to be ruined."

Amelia whimpered as she shook her head. "Please Ethan…."

Ethan ignored her, his thumb pressing down hard on her clit, rubbing in fast punishing circles that made her hips jerk against the mattress. The sensation burned too rough, too raw with sparks of pleasure colliding with searing humiliation.

"Don't squirm," he growled, his grip on her throat tightening just enough to keep her pinned beneath him. "Take it."

She gasped. Her nails dug into his wrists but that didn't stop him. His thumb worked her clit mercilessly, over and over until the line between pain and pleasure blurred and her thighs trembled around him.

"That's it," he hissed, leaning down to bite her bottom lip hard enough to draw blood.

"Fucking take it like the desperate little slut you are." His thumb circled her clit faster and harder. " This pussy is mine, say it."

Tears streaked her temples as she gasped for air.

"Say it, or I will rip another scream from your throat."

"Y…yours." she sobbed.

His smile curved against her cheek. "That's my good little whore."

He rubbed harder and faster. Her chest burning with sobs she couldn't voice.

"Come for me." he ordered, his voice dropping to a cold dangerous whisper. "Now."

She sobbed shaking her head but her body convulsed against her will. Heat and humiliation ripped through her all at once. Her orgasm tearing free with a cry strangled under his grip on her throat.

"That's it." He slowed but didn't stop. She twitched beneath him. "Look at you. Crying and coming at the same time. So fucking perfect."

Finally, he released her throat. She gasped, air rushing into her lungs so fast it made her chest ache. Her body trembled beneath him, her thighs still twitching with overstimulation and shock.

Ethan brushed his thumb across her lips, smearing her tears with a cruel tenderness.

"Don't worry baby. I'll always take care of you."

The echo of rain faded, replaced by the faint hum of the bathroom fan.

Amelia blinked, her vision refocusing on the present. Her phone buzzed on the bathroom counter. Her stomach lurched as she reached for it with trembling fingers.

Unknown number:

Do you remember how warm your skin got when you were afraid of me? I do

Her breath snagged in her throat. Another message :

I dreamed about your laugh last night. The real one. Before you started lying to me.

Another message popped up on the screen:

Soon.

The phone slipped from her fingers, cracking against the tile. The room wrapped around her, colours bleeding together as Ethan's breath filled her ear again:

Good girl. Stay still. Don't make me teach you again

Her chest seized. She clawed at her arms, desperate to scrape him off her skin and out of her soul. She didn't hear Lucas at first. His voice broke through with rough panic.

"Amelia?"

But she was already gone.

"Hey, baby, look at me. Amelia, it's me. You're safe."

Her body buzzed with terror, shaking like a wire about to snap. Blood welled from the raw scratches across her arms but he didn't feel it. She only felt the panic rising in her body.

"Amelia." Lucas's voice broke, hoarse and cracking. "You're not there. He's not here. It's me, just me."

Still nothing.

"Come back to me," he begged. "Please I'm right here."

Something in his voice cut through the screaming. Like a lifeline in the darkness.

She blinked once, twice.

"I can't" she whispered. He's still in me. I can't get him out."

Lucas pulled her into his lap, wrapping his arms around her.

"You're not his," he said fiercely. "Not anymore. You never were."

She buried her face in his neck, gasping like she was drowning. Like his scent was the only oxygen left in the world.

He rocked her gently, his warmth soaking into her bones.

"He doesn't get to win." Lucas whispered. "Not while I'm breathing."

.

Eight

Chapter 8

The office was warm.

Not comforting warm, it was more a suffocating warm. The kind that made her skin itch beneath her sweater sleeves.

She perched on the edge of the couch, spine rigid and arms crossed over her chest like armour.

Across from her, the therapist sat in an armchair, legs tucked to the side and notebook resting lightly on her knee. She didn't look judgemental. She didn't look impatient either. She just waited.

Amelia hated that.

"You don't have to say anything," the therapist said softly. "We can just sit here together if that feels safer."

Amelia said nothing. Her jaw clenched until her teeth ached. Silence stretched between them. The therapist didn't fill it. She simply watched, her gaze steady but gentle. As if reminding Amelia there was no rush.

"You've been through something no one should ever have to endure," she said after a long moment.

Amelia's chest tightened. Her eyes flicked away, settling on the bookshelf by the window. A book spine read *Reclaiming Yourself.* The words made her stomach churn.

She swallowed hard. "I didn't survive," she rasped. "I just didn't die."

The therapist didn't flinch or contradict. "You're still here," she said softly. "That counts."

Amelia scoffed. Her eyes burned with tears, blurring the bookshelf. "Does it? Feels like….. feels like all I did was lose parts of myself. One by one. Until there was nothing left to save."

The therapist's pen tapped once against her notebook before stilling. "That's how trauma works," she said gently. "It fragments us. It makes us feel hollow. But the fragments aren't gone forever. They're just hidden. Waiting for safety to come back together."

Amelia's fingers tightened on her arms. Her throat felt like it was closing.

Eventually the words slipped out. "He didn't start with his hands."

The therapist looked up, meeting her eyes. "No," she said. "They rarely do."

"It was little things at first." Amelia whispered. "Comments. Rules. Making me feel crazy for saying no. For needing….air."

Tears slipped down her cheeks before she could stop them.

"I used to think I was lucky. That he wanted me so much he couldn't help it."

"Abusers often start with emotional control," the therapist

said. "They chip away at your reality. So when violence comes, you've already convinced it's your fault."

A sob clawed at Amelia's chest, but she swallowed it down. "I didn't even scream the first time," she whispered. "I was too busy apologising."

Amelia's shoulders trembled. "I keep thinking….if I'd just left the first time. If I'd fought harder. If I hadn't said yes to the first thing. Maybe…"

"You did what you had to do to survive," the therapist said quietly. "That doesn't make you weak. That makes you alive."

Amelia's face crumpled. Her arms wrapped even tighter around herself.

The therapist passed her a box of tissues, sliding it across the coffee table without breaking eye contact.

"Breathe with me," she said softly. "In…and out. Slowly."

Amelia tried. Her breath shuddered as she dragged it in and let it out.

"It's not just what he did," she croaked after a moment. "It's what he made me believe."

The therapist nodded. "What did he make you believe Amelia?"

"That I was lucky to be chosen. That I was too much for anyone else. That pain was… the price of being wanted."

She let out a bitter, humourless laugh. "He used to say I had a light inside me. That it drove him crazy. That he had to dim it just a little so I wouldn't burn everything down."

The therapist's eyes softened with sorrow. "Abusers resent the light they are drawn to. They don't want to share it. They just want to own it, to consume it."

Amelia stared down at her lap. Her fingers twisted in the hem of her sweater, tugging at loose threads until they snapped.

"I still feel him in me," she whispered, her voice cracking. "Like a stain I can't scrub out."

"You won't always. The stain fades slowly. But right now, your nervous system is screaming that the danger isn't over. That you're still in the fire."

"Sometimes I think I'd rather burn then feel this hollow."

The therapist paused, choosing her words with care. "Hollow can be filled again. Burnout takes longer."

Amelia let out a shaky exhale. Tears dripped silently onto her jeans.

"You're not broken Amelia. You're a body that's been screaming for safety and now it's finally being heard."

The words lodged deep in her chest, sharp and aching.

"Do you want to try a grounding exercise before you leave?" The therapist asked.

Amelia hesitated, then nodded.

"Good." The therapist said softly. "Start with five things you can see."

Amelia blinked, her vision blurry from the tears. "The bookshelf. Your shoes….. The lamp. The clock and the… the plant."

"Four things you can touch."

"My jeans. The couch. My hair. The tissue box."

"Good, now three things you can hear."

"The clock ticking. The rain and your voice."

"Two things you can smell."

Amelia inhaled shakily. "Your tea and the candle."

"And one thing you can taste."

She swallowed. "The mint I had before I came in."

"Good," the therapist said, her voice warm with quiet pride. "Very good. How does your body feel now?

Amelia breathed in and out. Her chest still ached but her feet felt a bit more like she was on solid ground.

"I …I feel here," she whispered.

"That's enough for today."

When the session ended, Amelia didn't rush to the door like she thought she would. She sat for a moment longer, her body slumped in exhaustion. She felt tired but also lighter in a way she didn't understand.

When she stepped into the waiting room, Lucas stood immediately, his shoulders were stiff with worry. His eyes scanned her face, dark with questions he didn't voice.

"Hey," he said softly.

Amelia stepped into his arms without hesitation. His warmth wrapped around her, solid and quiet.

He pressed a kiss to her temple and whispered, "Proud of you," into her hair.

Nine

Chapter 9

It started with a sound. Barely a ping. Lucas's eyes flickered to his computer screen, his brows furrowing. The monitor glowed dimly in the darkness of his office. A new message blinked in his inbox. One that had bypassed firewalls he'd built himself.

Encrypted and Anonymous.

When he opened it, his blood turned to ice.

No more hiding. I see you.

Attached: an image.

Amelia, asleep in his bed. Her hair splayed across the pillow like a halo. His arm curled protectively around her waist.

The time stamp sent a chill through his body. It had been taken last night. He stood quickly, the chair crashed to the floor behind him. Rage pulsed hot and violent in his veins as he tore open the door, stalking into the living room. His eyes scanned every window, every feed from the security cameras streaming across his phone. Nothing. No breaches, no alarms.

But someone had been here. Someone had *seen* them.

"Lucas?" Amelia's voice came from down the hall, soft with sleep.

He turned and saw her standing in the bedroom doorway, wearing one of his shirts, hair tousled and eyes blinking open against the dim light.

His chest ached with something dark and furious. He walked to her, putting his hands around her, his grip firm and grounding.

"We're increasing security," he said, his voice low. "Now."

She blinked up at him, confusion cutting through the fog in her gaze. "Why? What happened?"

"Someone got into my system and sent a message." He swallowed, forcing down the tremor in his chest. "It had a photo attached."

Her breath hitched, eyes wide and terrified.

"Of me?"

He nodded once. "Taken last night, in this apartment."

Her face drained of colour. Her knees buckled and he caught her before she fell.

"You're not leaving my sight. I let him get you once. I won't make that mistake again." He growled, his hold on her tightening.

Lucas made calls. His voice lethal and unrecognisable even to himself. Within hours, every line of digital and physical access was locked down. Guards stationed at every entrance. Security feeds doubled. Weapons checked and loaded. By the time the sun sank behind the city skyline, the penthouse had become a fortress.

But it didn't feel safe.

Not to her.

She ate dinner in silence, pushing food around her plate without tasting it. Her gaze flickered to the windows again and again. As if expecting Ethan to emerge from the darkness outside.

Lucas watched her from across the room, his chest aching with a grief he didn't have words for.

That night, while he was in his office, he heard the water turn on and the soft click of the bathroom door.

Minutes passed.

Then a sound. A muffled sob.

He was on his feet instantly as he rushed to the bathroom, his hand knocking on the door.

"Amelia?"

No answer. He twisted the handle and stepped inside.

Steam coiled around him, thick and choking. The shower was running, water pooled across the tiles, spilling from the lip of the glass cubicle.

She was sitting under the spray of water fully clothed. Her knees drawn to her chest, arms wrapped tight around them. Water pounded down over her, soaking her hair and clothes. Her body shook with silent sobs, each one tearing through her like it was killing her from the inside.

Lucas stepped into the shower without hesitation. The water drenched his clothes in seconds, plastering his shirt to his chest. His jeans heavy around his thighs. He didn't care. He dropped to his knees beside her and gathered her into his arms. She didn't resist. She folded into him, her face pressing into his chest. Her sobs were silent, shaking her ribs against his.

"I can't breathe," she choked out. Her voice raw and strangled.

"Lucas….I can't…."

"Then I'll breathe for you," he whispered fiercely, pressing his lips to her temple. "Breathe with me angel. In. Out. That's it. I've got you. I've fucking got you."

She gasped, her chest heaving as water streamed down over them both.

He rocked her slowly, cradling her like she was something holy and shattered all at once.

"I've got you." He murmured. "No one's touching you again. Not while I'm breathing."

Her sobs tore though her but he didn't try to silence them. He just held her and stayed until the water ran cold.

Eventually, he stood and turned off the water. He lifted her easily, cradling her dripping body against him. She didn't speak, she just curled closer to him as he carried her out, leaving wet footprints on the wood floor.

He laid her on the bed and wrapped her in a blanket. She grabbed his wrist before he could leave. Her fingers trembled, her eyes wide and glassy.

"Stay," she whispered.

"Always." Lucas sat on the edge of the bed, stroking her damp hair back from her face. Her breathing deepened, slowing into the rhythm of sleep. She didn't let go of his shirt. Even in sleep, her fist still curled into the fabric. He stayed until her eyes closed and her breath came quiet and even. But sleep didn't come for him.

He stared at the ceiling, feeling her warmth pressed against his leg, the weight of her trust anchoring him and slicing him open all at once.

Her phone buzzed on the nightstand.

A new message:
You look good soaking wet, sweetheart. Brings back memories.

Lucas read it twice. The rage that rose in him was silent and bottomless. He turned his head to look at Amelia's sleeping face. The fragile peace she'd fought so hard for. He turned back to his phone.

Ethan was still watching. And this time? He wasn't hiding.

Ten

Chapter 10

The glow of the monitors painted Lucas's face in cold, shifting blues. His fingers danced over the keyboard, each keystroke precise, predatory. Lines of code bled down the screen, peeling back layers of the prison's firewalls.

He tunnelled deeper until he reached the restricted logs. There buried in outgoing traffic from Ethan's block, a pattern emerged. One device with the same ID. Sending encrypted files out after lights out.

Personal account registered to: **Mark Vance.**

Lucas leaned back, the corner of his mouth curving into something too sharp to be a smile.

"Found you. You're dead," he murmured to himself.

Mark's apartment was small. A second floor walk up with peeling paint and the smell of stale cigarettes embedded into the walls. Lucas didn't knock. He stepped inside with the quiet ease of someone who had no intention of leaving unseen.

Mark was at the kitchen table, hunched over a betting slip, a half empty glass of whisky by his elbow. His head jerked up at the sound of the door clicking shut.

"Who the fuck…."

Lucas was on him before he finished the sentence. A fist in his hair, slamming his face into the table. Whisky spread across the wood in a widening pool. The smell sharp and sour in the air.

"You've been busy," Lucas said, his tone conversational but wrong. It was the kind of voice people used when they'd already decided how this was going to end.

"I don't…."

Lucas pulled his phone from his pocket and pressed play. Amelia's muffled sobs spilled into the room, the sound of water running in the background. The recording was short but the silence after made the air feel heavier.

"That's the sound you sold."

Mark's face twisted. "It was just money."

Lucas crouched so they were eye-level. "You have a daughter, don't you? Fourteen?"

Mark froze. His Adam's apple bobbed hard.

Lucas's tone softened, almost gentle. "Imagine someone feeding her to a man like Ethan. Imagine what I'd do to them." His hand tightened in Mark's hair, pulling until the man winced. "Now understand this, you're in his place."

"Wait. I can give you names and his drop points!"

"You think this is about *information*?" Lucas asked, his head tilting. "I can find out all the information I need. This is about balance."

He let go, only to grab Mark by the throat, forcing him back in the chair. He reached into his pocket and pulled out a knife. Its edge catching in the light.

"Please," he begged.

The blade slid in under Mark's ribs with slow, deliberate pressure. Mark sucked in air through his teeth, the sound thick and wet.

Lucas didn't blink. "You were inside my home without stepping foot in it. You breathed her air. You put her through hell. That's a death sentence."

Mark's hands scrabbled weakly at Lucas's wrists. Lucas pushed the knife in deeper, feeling the resistance of muscle give way.

He leaned in, his lips now by the guard's ear. "When she sleeps tonight, she'll have no idea you're cooling on the floor. That's the difference between us, Mark. I keep her safe. You sold her to a wolf."

Mark's legs jerked once, twice, then nothing.

Lucas eased him to the ground and wiped the blade on the man's shirt.

He didn't look back as he stepped into the hall, locking the door behind him like nothing had happened.

* * *

The elevator chimed softly and opened into the penthouse. The scent of the city still clung to him. Rain, exhaust and the faint trace of copper he hadn't been able to wash from his hands. He set his keys down, every movement precise and controlled.

Amelia was on the couch, a blanket bunched around her legs and the flicker of the muted TV painting her skin in restless shadows. She looked up the second he entered. No smile, just eyes that searched his face like she was looking for something he wouldn't name.

"You're late." Her tone soft.

He sank down beside her, close enough for his thigh to brush hers. "I had business."

Her gaze drifted to his hands. "Business that makes you hide your knuckles?"

Lucas stilled, realising too late that his thumb was curled over his fits, hiding the faint red along his skin. "Someone needed a reminder," he said.

Her brows pulled together. "And you were the reminder?"

A slow, dangerous smiled curved his mouth. "I was the consequence."

She didn't recoil, didn't look away. Instead she shifted curling into his side. "And what did they do to deserve you?"

"They made the mistake of thinking you were unprotected."

For a moment, her breath caught. Not in fear but in something heavier. Her fingers toyed with the hem of his shirt. "You can't keep doing that forever, Lucas."

His hand cupped her jaw, tilting her face to meet his eyes. "Yes, I can and I will. Until there's nothing left in me but the will to keep you breathing."

She swallowed hard but didn't pull away. "That's obsession."

"Maybe," he breathed, brushing his lips against her hair. "But it's the only thing keeping him from taking you again."

They stayed like that, silent but not at peace. Amelia's

heartbeat slowed against him but her mind didn't. She could feel it, the edge in him tonight. It was sharper then usual like whatever he'd done hadn't burned the fury out of him. It only fanned it.

When she finally looked up, his eyes were already on her. Dark and steady.

"Tell me it was worth it," she whispered.

He didn't hesitate. "It always is."

Eleven

Chapter 11

The next morning dawned grey and heavy. The kind of day that blurred the line between waking and dreaming.

Amelia hadn't spoken much since the night before. Lucas hadn't expected her to. He moved quietly through the penthouse, close but not crowding her. The faint trace of copper still clung to his skin, no matter how many times he'd washed his hands.

By late afternoon, rain fell against the windows. Soft and steady. Amelia sat curled in a chair, a blanket draped over her legs.

Lucas approached, slow and careful.

"Mind if I sit with you?"

She didn't answer right away but then she nodded once. He lowered himself beside her, leaving a breath of space between them. Silence stretched thick but gentle.

She turned her head, her eyes tired but not empty.

"Will you touch me?" She asked.

Lucas stilled. "Amelia…. you don't have to…."

"Not like that," she cut in quickly, shaking her head. "I just… I want to feel safe in my skin again. I want to feel like it's mine. And you…you never made me feel owned. Even when I gave myself to you."

His jaw flexed. "What do you need from me?"

She swallowed, gaze drifting down. "Lie down with me. Just touch me. Anywhere. Everywhere. I want to remember what it feels like when it doesn't hurt."

He nodded, rising and offering her his hand. She took it, her fingers were cool against his palm.

He led her to the bedroom without words. Only the hush of rain and the quiet rhythm of their breaths filled the space between them.

She crawled onto the mattress, lying on her back and her eyes wide open. Vulnerable but not afraid.

Lucas knelt beside her, giving her a moment to settle into the moment. "Can I start with your hands?"

She nodded.

He took her hand gently in his, holding it between both of his palms. Slowly, he traced circles over her skin. Across her palm, along each finger and down to her wrist.

"Tell me if anything feels wrong."

"I will," she whispered.

He moved to her other hand, pressing soft kisses to each knuckle. Her breathing slowed, the tension easing from her shoulders.

"You always did this," she murmured. "Before. When I was

nervous. You'd touch me like I was something fragile…. even when you wanted to ruin me."

His eyes met hers, dark and endless. "Because even then, I loved *every* crack you tried to hide."

She blinked fast, tears catching in her lashes. "Keep going."

He moved up to her arms. His fingertips skimming from wrist to elbow then to her shoulder. Just enough pressure to ground her without overwhelming.

Her eyes fluttered closed.

"You okay?"

"Yes," she breathed. "More please."

He pushed the blanket down to her waist, sliding his palms over her abdomen in slow quiet strokes. Through the thin cotton of her shirt, he felt her breaths flutter. He didn't push further, instead he circled his thumb in gentle arcs above her navel, then pressed his palm flat over her belly.

"Breathe here," he whispered. "Into my hand."

She obeyed, her belly rising and falling. Lucas leaned down, pressing a soft kiss to her shoulder.

He slid his hand beneath the hem of her shirt, resting his palm against the warm skin of her ribs. She stiffened then exhaled.

"Don't stop."

When her muscles loosened beneath his touch, he stroked slowly up her side and back down. Grounding her in the rhythm.

Her eyes opened. "I want you to tell me what to do."

Lucas paused. "Amelia…"

"Just something small," she said, her voice shaking but sure. "Not because I'm submitting. Not yet. Just because I want to remember what it feels like to obey and not feel afraid."

His chest ached, but there was steel under the ache. The same steel that had slid a knife under a man's ribs twelve hours ago.

"Close your eyes and keep breathing just like that for me."

She followed him. In and out.

"Now turn onto your side."

She shifted slowly and he moved in behind her. His chest warm against her back.

"Put your hand over mine."

She reached back, lacing her fingers with his.

"Good girl," his tone low, dangerous and threaded with possession.

She froze but then shivered. The words that used to cut her open, now stitched her back together.

"That okay?"

"Yes," she whispered. "Say it again."

"Good girl."

A trembling breath fell from her lips. It wasn't from fear but from release. They stayed like that for a long time, rain whispering against the glass. Finally, she spoke, her voice soft but steady.

"When I'm ready…. I want you to take me apart again. Not because I need to be broken but because I want to see how far I've come.

Lucas closed his eyes, tightening his hold on her. "When your ready, I will worship every piece of you. And I'll destroy anyone who ever tries to touch what's mine."

Chapter 12

By midday, Lucas's phone wouldn't stop buzzing. Once. Twice. Again.

Amelia set her mug down, pulse thudding in her ears. "Answer it," she said, voice sharper then she meant for.

He answered without moving from her side, voice clipped, each word edged with steel. Amelia watched the change in him, the softness from last night bleeding out of his face until only the predator remained.

He hung up, sliding the phone onto the table. His gaze found hers.

"Sophia's on her way up."

"Why?"

"They're not waiting for the hearing," he said, jaw tight. "Ethan's team just filed an emergency appeal. They're pushing for early review."

Amelia blinked. "That's not possible. The hearing isn't even here yet."

"They're claiming judicial bias. Media interference. And…" his voice dropped. "They're painting you as unstable."

Her stomach lurched. "They used my breakdown. didn't they?"

Lucas's silence was answer enough.

"Tell me," she pushed.

"It leaked. The footage of you being carried out of the courtroom."

Air punched out of her lungs. "God, everyone saw me like that."

"They won't win." He said.

A knock split the moment.

Amelia walked across the room before he could. When she opened the door, Sophia stood there, umbrella dripping, eyes wide.

"Oh honey,"

Amelia fell into her arms like gravity had been waiting.

On the couch, Sophia pulled her close, rocking her as if nothing had changed since college. "Talk to me."

"They're calling me unstable," Amelia whispered. "Weak. Unfit to stand."

Sophia cupped her face. "They're liars. You broke in public, sure. That doesn't make you weak. It makes you human."

"I gave them proof."

"You gave them nothing," Sophia shot back. "You let yourself feel. That's not proof of weakness. That's proof you're still alive."

Lucas leaned forward in the chair opposite the girls. "We'll counter. Witness, medical records whatever we need to do. They won't touch you again."

Sophia's eyes cut to him. "She doesn't just need a legal defence. She needs a strategy. A war room."

"I'll build one." Lucas said.

"No," Amelia interrupted. Her voice didn't shake this time. "We will. All of us. I'm done being carried. If they want a fight, I'll give them one."

Sophia smiled. "That's my girl."

Lucas studied her, hunger and pride filling his eyes. "Once we start, Amelia, there's no undoing it."

"Good." Her chin lifted. "Then let's make me unstoppable."

* * *

Later that night, Lucas led her into the bedroom, but the energy had shifted. This wasn't comfort. This was preparation.

"May I kneel, Sir?" She asked.

His chest tightened. "You may."

She sank to the floor. Not fragile. Not prey but whole and ready.

"Colour?" His voice low and steady.

"Green."

"Tell me why you're here."

Her nails dug lightly into her thighs, her breath catching. "To remind myself my body is mine. Submission is mine."

Lucas's gaze burned down her spine. "Pain?"

A shiver rippled through her but she shook her head. "No, not yet."

"Bound?"

Her pulse thudded in her ears. "No."

"Guide you?"

She lifted her chin, meeting his gaze. "Yes, Sir."

He stepped behind her and placed a blindfold over her eyes. Darkness closed around her like armour.

"Breathe with me."

She matched his breath, her pulse slowed and sharpened.

"Say your name." He commanded.

Her lips parted. "Amelia." The sound trembled.

"Say who you are."

Her lungs burned. The words scraped up from somewhere buried. "I am a survivor."

"Again."

Her spine straightened, muscles taut. "I am a survivor." Stronger this time.

His hands slid up to cradle her face. Calloused thumbs brushing her damp skin. "And what else?"

Her jaw locked, fire in her throat. "I am not his."

"Louder." His demand cut through the air.

Her chest heaved, and she let it rip free like a scream she'd be swallowing for years.

"I am not his!"

The words scorched her tongue, raw and searing. It left her shaking but also lighter, like something had finally broken loose inside her.

Lucas kissed her knuckles. "You are mine, only because you choose and you can choose again. Always."

Tears fell behind the blindfold. "I want this. Not because I'm broken but because I'm rebuilding. And because I will not let him win."

"Then I'll hold every brick, every scar and every tremor, until the world knows you cannot be touched." Lucas said as he took of the blindfold.

"Tell me what to do." She whispered as her eyes adjusted to the light.

His mouth curved slow and dangerous. "Careful baby. Don't ask for what you're not ready to handle."

Her pulse raced but she lifted her chin to meet his gaze. "I wouldn't ask if I couldn't take it."

For a moment, silence burned between them. Then his voice dropped, rough with restraint.

"Then take it." He caught her wrist and pressed her palm against him, the thick length pressing against his trousers.

Her pulse thundered. For a heartbeat she froze but then her fingers found his zipper. When she freed him, his cock sprang heavy and hot into her hand. The veins pulsing against her palm.

Amelia sank to her knees, one hand curling tight around the base and the other bracing against his thigh. She brushed her lips over the head, tasting the salty precum that was glistening.

"Fuck, Amelia.." His breath hissed. His hips jerking forward.

She wrapped her mouth around him, sliding down his cock until the head hit the back of her throat. Drool spilling from her lips and her jaw aching as she pushed deeper.

Lucas groaned, fingers fisting in her hair. "God, you're so fucking perfect. Look at you on your knees for me."

Her throat clenched around him, making him curse. He guided her faster and rougher until she gagged on him, tears sliding down her cheeks. She moaned around his cock, the sound vibrating through him.

"Good girl," he growled, his voice breaking as the release hit. Hot, thick spurts filled her mouth and she swallowed every drop, licking the tip clean before pulling off with a wet gasp.

She looked up at him, lips swollen and eyes blazing.

"On the bed," he ordered. His voice sharp and dark. "Spread that pretty pussy for me."

She obeyed, rising with shaky legs and lying back against the sheets. Lucas peeled her underwear down slow, dragging it over her thighs like a man savouring every inch.

Her legs fell open for him, her pussy wet and glistening. His low curse vibrated against her skin as he bent down, kissing down her neck, across her breasts. Leaving sharp nips in his wake, His hand slid between her thighs, his fingers pressing into her pussy, curling until her hips bucked.

"Lucas please…" She moaned.

He stroked her clit with his thumb watching as she trembled. "Not yet. You're going to come on my cock."

Her whimper turned desperate when he finally pushed his cock inside her. Stretching her open in one deep, punishing thrust.

"Fuck you're so tight and perfect." He groaned, pressing his forehead to hers.

Her nails clawed down his back as he began to move. Slow at first then harder and deeper driving the air from her lungs with every thrust. The sound of their bodies colliding filled the room, wet and relentless.

"Say it," he growled, biting her shoulder. "Tell me who you belong to."

Her eyes rolled back, her orgasm building like fire in her veins. "I'm yours," she cried out.

Her back arched off the bed, pleasure clawing up her spine. "OMG! I'm going to fucking come!" She screamed.

"That's it baby," Lucas groaned, slamming harder and faster. "Come for me. Come all over my cock."

Her climax ripped through her like a detonation. He fucked her through it, dragging her higher and wringing every aftershock out of her until she was shaking beneath him.

"Fuck…." His growl cracked as his own orgasm overtook him. He spilled hot inside her, grinding deep, emptying himself as her name left his lips.

"You feel that?" he murmured, pressing deeper and grinding so she felt every inch of him still inside her. "That's mine. Now and forever. Not because I took it. But because you gave it."

Her hands curled over his forearm, nails digging lightly into his skin, "I wanted to. I *needed* to."

He kissed the side of her throat, slow and claiming. "Good girl. You fought for this. You fought for me and for us. And now…." His tone dropped dark and deliberate. "Now we take that fight outside these walls"

Her body still shuddered with the aftershocks but her voice was steady when she whispered. "I'm ready."

Lucas pulled out slowly then rolled her onto her side and caged her with his body. One arm banded across her waist. His cock still hard against her ass. He held her like a shield and a threat all in one.

He kissed her shoulder. "Rest tonight. Tomorrow we make war."

Amelia's lips curved into a small dangerous smile.

In the mirror across the room, her reflection stared back at her. Sweat-slick, flushed with a fire in her eyes.

For the first time, she believed it. She wasn't broken, she wasn't prey. She was ready to burn the world down.

Thirteen

Chapter 13

The morning light was almost kind. Almost.

The kitchen still smelled faintly of cloves and cinnamon. Lucas's blend made hours ago and abandoned in the French press when neither of them had been able to eat. Amelia sat at the long dinning table that faced the floor-to-ceiling windows of the penthouse.

Amelia wore one of Lucas's black hoodies, the sleeves pulled over her hands, bare legs curled beneath her. She looked almost peaceful.

Lucas watched from the open kitchen. Mug in hand, unread email glowing on his tablet. But all his attention was on her.

There was a softness to her this morning, but not weakness. A quiet earned through fire. She'd made a list of goals last night. Small, steady things. Cook breakfast, without shaking, answer a few emails and maybe even call her therapist.

Healing, he was learning, didn't come with lightning bolts.

It came with moments like this, her whispering good morning like a vow. Her breath steady and her gaze clear.

He was about to speak when the intercom buzzed.

Lucas's jaw tensed.

Amelia looked up. "It's okay," she said quietly. "Let her in."

He crossed to the panel and pressed the button. "Morning, Sophia."

Her voice crackled through. "Tell her not to panic, but I'm coming up. And she needs to see this. Right now."

The elevator took twenty seconds. Lucas watched each one tick by on the panel, his pulse quickening. Sophia didn't alarm easily.

The elevator doors opened directly into the penthouse.

"Sophia what…" Amelia started, but her best friend didn't greet her with words.

Sophia strode across the marble floor, rain soaked, coat half-unbuttoned, eyes wide and burning.

"Where's your phone?" She demanded.

Amelia blinked, startled. "Still in the bedroom, why?"

Sophia didn't wait, she dropped her tablet onto the dining table in front of her.

Lucas moved beside them in an instant. He didn't have to see the screen to feel the shift in the room.

The screen was paused on a still image. It was grainy, shadowed but unmistakably real.

Amelia's face.

On her knees.

Looking up.

Exclusive: Courtroom Victim or Willing Submissive? Leaked Footage Raises New Questions About Amelia Monroe

She didn't move, not at first. Her breath caught but didn't release. The tremor started in her fingertips.

Sophia's voice dropped to a whisper. "Don't read the comments. Don't watch it again. You don't need to…"

Amelia reached forward and tapped the screen to press play.

The video began with static.

A long hallway. Dim lighting. A hotel room, maybe. Cheap and familiar.

A door opened and there she was.

Younger and frailer. Pale skin bruised at the shoulder, a fading mark along her jaw. Obvious now but easily missed then. She was wearing a long grey T-shirt and nothing underneath.

Barefoot. Kneeling. Obedient.

Amelia couldn't remember who held the camera. But she remembered the night. She hadn't wanted to be filmed. She had said no, she even begged but Ethan had told her this was proof. That she wanted it, that she liked it when he called her his little slut. That no one would believe her if she tried to say otherwise.

Now the world was watching and the edit was merciless.

Her voice trembled. "Please…Ethan."

Audio distortion. Caption overlay. **Playful Begging.**

The cut jumped.

She was on her knees the same frame, closer to the camera now. Eyes glassy, cheeks flushed and her hair roughly pulled aside.

He slapped her.

Not a BDSM- safe, practised strike. A backhand, clumsy and full of spite.

But the video blurred the motion. Paused just before the contact. Then resumed only when she was lowering her head.

Caption: Power exchange or abuse? You decide.

The room spun.

Amelia stared at the screen, frozen. She didn't even realise her nails were digging into her thighs until Lucas's hand gently covered hers.

"You don't have to keep watching," he said, his voice low.

"I do."

The video kept going.

A moment where Ethan's voice rang out clearly:

"Say you love it, Amelia."

Her answer, choked and mechanical:

"I love it."

She remember that moment, remembered how it had come after a choke hold. After two hours of being pushed face- down into the mattress and told she was nothing unless she *proved* she could take it. She had said the words to survive.

But now the world heard them as a confession.

Audio overlay: **Consent culture under scrutiny. When kink goes too far, who draws the line?**

A media experts voice cut in.

"It's clear she was involved in a power exchange dynamic. The question is whether she regretted it later and re framed it as assault."

"She was *beaten*," Sophia spat. "There are *medical* records."

Lucas didn't speak. His jaw clenched so hard the vein in his neck pulsed.

The screen flickered again.

A final still image.

Amelia, curled at the base of a bed, completely naked. Covered in bruises, one arm shielding her chest and her eyes shut. Defeated.

"Screenshot from alleged 'abuse' or aftermath of a consensual scene?"

Breaking: Legal Analysts Weighs In on Amelia's Emotional Instability and the Reliability of Victim Testimony in the Age of Kink Culture.

Amelia stood up so suddenly her chair screeched backward. She didn't run to the bathroom. Didn't collapse. She crossed the room and stared out at the rain-slicked skyline.

For a long moment she said nothing.

Rain streaked down the glass like tears too exhausted to fall properly.

The world below blurred, city lights smeared like watercolour bleeding in too much water.

No one spoke.

Behind her, Sophia had lowered herself slowly into a chair, face pale with fury. Lucas remained standing, arms folded across his chest, his eyes fixed on Amelia like he could anchor her through sheer will.

"You need to get ahead of it," Sophia said finally. "We can call Andrea from The Guardian. she's solid, feminist, smart and not afraid to go after media vultures."

"Already done." Lucas replied. "She's holding the story until Amelia says she's ready."

The word, consent, hung in the air like a cracked bell.

Amelia exhaled slowly. Her voice, when it came was quiet. But no longer shaking.

"He made me say those things," she said. "I was dissociating. I couldn't feel my hands, my skin felt like it wasn't mine."

Sophia's voice broke. "I know. We know."

Amelia turned from the window, her eyes were dry and her face was stone.

"They are going to eat it alive. The media. The podcasts. The lawyers. They are going to call me a liar. A slut. A sub who changed her mind and cried wolf."

"Let them try," Lucas said stepping toward her. "We'll destroy them."

"No," she said sharply. "*I* will."

The words snapped through the room like a crack of lightning.

Sophia looked up, startled. Lucas stilled.

"I'm done hiding," Amelia said. "Done apologising for surviving. They want to use my bruises as proof I asked for it? Fine. Let them see all of it. Let them see the difference between consent and coercion."

Lucas's jaw flexed. "You don't owe them your trauma."

"I don't," she agreed. "But I do owe myself the truth. Told out loud and without shame."

Sophia rose and came to her. "You're going to need a strategy. A team. You're already trending on social media and it's vicious out there."

"Then I'll be vicious too."

Lucas stepped closer. "You're not alone in this. You want to go public? You want to reclaim the narrative? Then we do it together."

Amelia looked up at him. "I want to go to war," she whispered. "But I want to do it as your submissive."

For a beat, Lucas stilled. Her words sinking deep, breaking through every wall he'd built

His hand rose slowly, wrapping around her throat, not in cruelty but with reverent possession. His grip tightened just enough to make her feel it, to anchor her to him.

Something flickered in his gaze. Pride, hunger and devotion so raw it almost looked like ruin.

"Then you'll go to war as mine," he murmured. "My submissive. My weapon. My everything.

Behind them Sophia was already opening her laptop. "I'll call Andrea. We'll write it together. You'll control the language, the frame the timing. They won't spin this."

Lucas turned slightly. "I want full encryption. No leaks, I don't trust half the legal system right now."

Sophia nodded." I know someone. I'll vet everyone who touches the file.

Amelia looked between them.

"I want the world to hear it in my voice," she said. "Not some watered- down statement. I want to speak it on video."

Lucas stilled. "You sure?"

Amelia nodded. "I'm done being a headline. I want to be the fucking story."

Fourteen

Chapter 14

The living room became a battlefield.

Sophia sat cross-legged on the couch, laptop open and her fingers moving fast across the keyboard. Multiple tabs open: news articles, social media feeds, PR contacts and legal code. She looked like she hadn't blinked in ten minutes.

Lucas stood near the window, phone to his ear, his voice low. The skyline stretched behind him like a storm waiting to be summoned.

Amelia sat between them. Still in his hoodie, still barefoot. But everything about her posture had shifted. Her spine was straight and her eyes clear. There was something dangerous about her calm.

"They've already picked it up in syndication," Sophia said without looking up from her laptop. "Fox, TMZ, even some pseudo-academic kink forums. The discourse is spiralling. They're turning your abuse into a case study for 'miscommunication in BDSM'."

Amelia didn't flinch.

"I want to go live. Not a pre-recorded video. No editing."

Sophia's fingers paused. "That's a big risk."

"I want them to see my face when I talk about what he did. I want them to see I'm not ashamed anymore."

Lucas ended the call and walked over, sliding his phone onto the table.

"My legal contact says Ethan's team leaked the footage through a third party. They used a VPN and bounced it through proxies. But it originated from someone in his camp. We'll never get a clean trail."

"Of course not," Sophia muttered. "He's building a case for his appeal. Trying to re frame the narrative before sentencing hits."

Amelia looked at Lucas. "How much time could he get reduced if this works?"

Lucas's jaw tightened. "Too much."

"OK then I want my video up by tomorrow night."

Lucas sat beside her. "We need media prep. Controlled lighting and a legal script that says enough without giving them ammunition."

Amelia turned to face him fully.

"No script."

He blinked. "Amelia…."

"I don't want to be polished. I don't want to be managed. I want to be real. You don't get to tell me to filter myself."

He reached over, gently curling his fingers around her wrist.

"You're mine," he said, his voice rough.

Amelia stilled.

"And because you're mine, I'll protect you even from the fire you're ready to walk into."

Sophia coughed pointedly. "You two want me to leave the room while you growl at each other or….?"

Amelia smirked. The first shadow of a smile since the footage hit.

"We're fine."

Lucas leaned in. His voice was for her ears only. "You're not my property but you are my responsibility."

Her breath hitched.

"And you want to fight this as my submissive," he continued. "Then we fight it my way. That means preparation and control."

She nodded slowly. "Fine. But you don't own the narrative. I do."

A beat passed then Lucas smiled. It wasn't a soft smile, it was full of teeth.

* * *

By the evening, the penthouse no longer felt like a sanctuary. It felt more like a bunker.

Sophia had pulled in two vetted contacts. One a security adviser and the other a PR strategist. Both women, both survivors themselves. They sat around the long marble island in the kitchen, listening as Amelia laid out exactly what she wanted to say.

"I want to open with the footage," she said. "Fifteen seconds, just enough to show the moment he slapped me. Then cut to me. No voice over. No commentary."

"Powerful." The strategist nodded. "Painful but powerful."

"I want to say his name. Ethan Walker. I want to tell people what he did to me, what I thought love was and how he used kink as cover for violence."

The adviser frowned. "There will be backlash. People in the kink community will feel attacked."

"Then they should speak up to," Amelia said. "The ones who understand consent. Who protect their subs. Let them stand beside me."

Lucas watched her speak.

Watched her reclaim every piece of herself with no apology.

He could feel his heart tightening. His hands aching to touch her.

Later, he promised himself. When the world was quiet.

Hours passed. Guests left, promises had been exchanged and plans finalised.

The penthouse dimmed. Sophia had gone to bed in the guest suite. Only Lucas and Amelia remained. The silence stretching thick between them.

She stood by the window again, arms wrapped around herself. Not from fear this time but from the weight of what she'd chosen to do.

Lucas approached slowly.

"You were fierce tonight," he said.

"I didn't cry."

"You didn't need to." He reached out his hand on her jaw, turning her head to face him.

"I saw you," he whispered. "Every part of you and it made me want to do something I have never done with anyone else. It made me want to kneel for you."

Her throat tightened. "I wanted to beg for the chance to serve the woman who stood in that room and refused to be erased." Lucas leaned in, his forehead resting against hers.

"You burned so bright I forgot I was supposed to protect you."

Amelia closed her eyes. "I'm scared," she whispered. "But I want this."

"I know."

Her throat worked around the word. "Sir."

Lucas inhaled sharply.

"I'm still yours," she said. "Even in the war."

His reply wasn't words. His mouth crashed against hers, a kiss so fierce it stole the ground out from under her. Her back hit the wall with a thud, his hand sliding into her hair.

"Especially in the war." He growled against her mouth.

The storm inside her didn't break, it burned hotter. Dread, anger and hunger coiled tight, twisting into need. His hoodie hung loose on her, and when his fingers found the hem, she let him drag it up, baring her skin to the cool air.

They staggered down the hallway, kissing like it was oxygen. His hand firm at her throat, hers fisting in his shirt. Every step was a stumble, a surrender, a declaration. By the time the bedroom door hit the wall, her pulse was everywhere. Her fingertips, her throat, and between her thighs.

Lucas tore at the bed, stripping it down to nothing but the dark fitted sheet and the rug at the base. His chest rising hard, his eyes never leaving her.

Amelia sank slowly to her knees on the rug and when she looked up at him, her lips swollen, her breath unsteady, she whispered, " Yours."

She stayed kneeling on the rug, her chest rising and falling. When Lucas finally spoke, his voice was low and steady. "Colour?

Her lips parted. "Green."

He moved to the drawer without breaking her gaze, pulling out the leather paddle. The weight of it in his hand made her pulse race. When he came back to her, he didn't rush. He dragged the paddle across her skin first, testing, teasing before snapping it against her thigh.

She gasped then moaned as heat bloomed where it landed. Another strike. Then another. The sound cracked through the air, the ache melting into pleasure until her body shuddered with it.

"On the bed," he ordered.

She obeyed, crawling up onto the stripped mattress, her skin flushed and her breath shaky. He caught her wrists, binding them to the headboard.

"Legs apart," he whispered in her ear.

Her pulse thundered, as she spread for him. His hand slid down, fingers circling her clit.

His mouth curved into a dark smile. "So wet for me already."

Her breath hitched when his first finger pressed inside her, slow and unrelenting.

"One," he murmured, staring into her eyes.

A moan tore from her throat.

The second slid in beside it, stretching her further. His eyes never leaving her gaze.

"Two."

Her back bowed off the bed, another moan spilling louder.

He twisted his wrists just slightly and the third finger

entered.

"Three."

Her thighs shook against the sheets. "Lucas….."

"Sir." He corrected, pushing deeper and watching her unravel.

"Sir." She gasped her voice breaking.

A fourth finger filled her, his knuckles pressing her open, his pace deliberate and merciless.

"Four."

Her cry echoed off the walls, her hips jerking off the bed,

Then he gave her the fifth, his entire hand claiming her.

"Five."

The sound she made was raw, almost feral as her body fought and yielded all at once. She was writhing, hips jerking off the bed, sweat streaking her temples and her moans a chorus that only drove him harder.

Her voice cracked high and desperate. "I….oh god… I'm going to…"

His lips brushed her ear, his growl a command that split her in two. "Let go. Feel it all."

The dam inside her broke. The release was violent, unstoppable. Tearing through her until her body arched and convulsed around him. Heat and wetness spilled over his hand.

Lucas's stilled, eyes dark with shock and hunger. His voice rough. "Did you just fucking squirt?"

Amelia's face burned, shame flickering through the haze of bliss. "Oh my god I've never…."

He caught her chin, forcing her eyes to him. "Don't you dare be embarrassed. It's the hottest thing I've ever seen."

Then his belt hit the floor, his pants sliding away and he was positioning himself between her thighs. He thrust into her in one brutal stroke, stretching her open around the thick weight of him. Amelia's scream split the air.

"Fuck," Lucas snarled driving deeper. "You take me so well every inch."

Her wrists strained against the headboard as he filled her, the thick length of him bottoming out until she could feel him everywhere. She moaned breathless. "God, you're so big."

He drew back slow, almost cruel before slamming back inside, hips colliding hers hard enough to rattle the bed frame. His cock pounding into her, relentless. The heavy drag of it forcing louder cries from her throat. He watched her face twist, her body shudder and it only fed the hunger tearing through him.

Every thrust was deep, punishing but his voice was raw. "No one will ever fuck you like this. No one will ever fit you like I do."

When he grounded his hips against hers, the thick head of his cock hitting deep inside, her cry turned ragged, her body clenching hard around him. He groaned, jaw tight, sweat dripping from his temple.

"Come on my cock baby," he ordered, this thumb reaching between them and circling her clit. "I want to feel you gush for me."

Her scream broke, her body spasming around him. Wetness flooding as she shattered. Lucas's curse tore free as he felt her clench, the tight spasms dragging him closer, harder until his release ripped through him with a groan that shook his entire body.

He spilled deep inside her, thrusting through it, filling her until he was sure she'd never forget what it meant to be claimed.

When he collapsed against her, his cock still thick and pulsing inside her, his breath was ragged. "Mine. You're fucking mine."

Fifteen

Chapter 15

The room was still humming with the echoes of them. Sweat, breath and the faint sting of leather still on her thighs. Lucas's weight pressed warmly against her. His heartbeat slowing where his chest touched her back.

Then her phone buzzed. Lucas tensed beside her. "Don't," he said softly. "It can wait."

But it couldn't.

She rose slowly. One notification. A single alert.

Breaking News: Ethan Walker's Legal Team Files Formal Appeal Based on New Evidence.

She opened the article.

There it was. In black and white.

"Mr Walker's defence team argues that recently surfaced footage demonstrates a pattern of consensual behaviour, casting doubt on

Ms. Monroe's claims of non-consensual abuse.

The defence also questions Ms. Monroe's mental stability and potential media motivations for pursuing high profile litigation."

The article included a side by side image. One from the leaked footage. One of her sobbing outside the courtroom on the day of the verdict.

As if the contrast proved contradiction.

As if her pain had to fit their mould to be believed.

Behind her, Lucas was already pulling on a hoodie.

"What is it?" he asked.

She turned to him, holding out the phone.

He read it once. His jaw locked. Then he looked at her. Not like she was fragile and not like she might break but like she might *burn the whole damn world down.*

Amelia handed him the phone, then walked to the closet. She pulled out her favourite dark green sweater. The one she used to wear when she needed armour and slipped it on. Then leggings and then her boots.

She turned to Lucas as she tied her hair back.

"I'm ready."

"For what?" he asked.

"To film."

He blinked. "Tonight?"

She nodded. "Before they get to define me again. Before the world writes another headline about my body and calls it evidence."

Lucas crossed the room to her.

"Let me speak to your team first," he said. "We'll lock down location, sound, lighting...."

"No lighting," she interrupted. "No makeup, no edits just me. One camera. One shot. Tonight."

Lucas hesitated, then searched her face and saw the unshakeable truth in her eyes.

She was done hiding. She didn't just want to survive. She wanted to win.

"Then I'll set it up."

"Tonight," she whispered.

Sixteen

Chapter 16

The room was stripped bare. They'd chosen the library as the backdrop for the video.

No art. No distractions. No performance.

Just Amelia.

Lucas stood behind the camera, silent and watchful. Sophia sat on the floor just out of frame, her laptop open and ready to manage the upload the second Amelia gave the word. The other, PR, legal, and security were on standby. But no one else was allowed in the room.

Amelia sat in the chair her hands folded on her lap. No makeup and her hair tied back.

She didn't look fragile, she looked like a blade.

Lucas adjusted the camera. He met her eyes once. "Whenever you're ready."

Amelia nodded and then he pressed record.

Silence for a moment then her voice. Low and steady.

Intimate in a way that cut deeper than any shouted defence ever could.

"My name is Amelia Monroe."

No tremble. No apology.

"I'm the woman in the footage." She let the pause stretch. Let the viewers sit with the reality of it. No denial. No shame.

"That video was taken without my consent. It was edited without my knowledge. And it's being used now in an attempt to dismantle my credibility and reduce the sentence of the man who raped me."

Lucas's hands curled into fists at his side. But he didn't move.

Amelia continued.

"I was in a relationship with Ethan Walker. When we met, he was kind, charismatic and charming. I didn't see what was underneath. He never hit me at first. Never raised his voice. That came later, slowly like poison. A little more each day.

Her breath deepened. Steady.

"I want to be clear about something. What Ethan did to me wasn't BDSM. It wasn't kink. It wasn't part of any negotiated dynamic. I wasn't a submissive. I was a girlfriend. A woman in love and he used that love to break me down until I didn't recognise myself."

Her voice wavered, just once but she caught it. Breathed through it and let the silence hold her steady.

"I've since chosen to explore submission, consensually and safely with someone I trust. But that choice has nothing to do with what Ethan did. There was no safe word. There was no consent. There was only control. Pain and fear."

Lucas stared at her through the lens. But he wasn't seeing her on camera. He was seeing her *become* something fierce and whole. And inside his chest, something split open.

Amelia leaned forward slightly. "There are people watching this who will call me dramatic. A liar. A woman who changed her mind and wants to punish a man for something she once said yes to."

She blinked, slowly.

"To those people, I say this; yes I said yes, to Ethan being in my life. Until I didn't and he didn't stop."

Lucas's breath caught.

Amelia's gaze burned straight into the camera now.

"And to the women watching this who see pieces of themselves in me. Who have footage or text messages, or even photos that you know they'll use against you. I see you. I believe you. You're not alone. You're not shame."

The silence that followed felt holy.

Then:

"I was broken," she whispered. "But I rebuilt. Not into something softer. Into something stronger. I am not afraid of my truth anymore."

She sat back and let the words breathe.

"My name is Amelia Monroe and I survived."

She looked into the lens for two more seconds then gave Lucas a single nod.

He clicked stop. No one spoke, not for a long time.

Sophia exhaled, closed her laptop and left the room silently. Respect in every step.

Lucas approached slowly, the air between them thick with devotion.

"You didn't just survive," he said. "You fucking rose."

Amelia's eyes met his.

"I needed to say it out loud. I needed to own it."

He stepped closer, his hand brushing hers.

"Let me say something now," he murmured. "Just for you."

She tilted her head. "What?"

He looked at her like she was something he'd spent his whole life trying to protect but only just realised he'd needed to worship.

"You're not what he made of you."

She closed her eyes, holding the words against her chest like a secret.

Then whispered. "Then help me show the world what I really am."

The video dropped at 7:03 AM. By 7:08, it was trending worldwide.

#ISeeYouAmelia

#ConsentIsChoice

#AmeliaMonroeSpeaks

The penthouse glowed blue with the light of multiple screens. Phones, laptops, tablets and the television in the corner playing a muted news feed with her face in the lower third. Amelia sat on the couch, untouched by the noise.

Calm. Not detached though. Present, watching it all happen.

Sophia sat beside her, furiously fielding calls and emails. Every time a notification popped up, she scrolled faster. "New Times wants a quote. Every blog and news station is talking about it."

She looked over at Amelia. "You broke the internet, babe."

Amelia didn't smile but she didn't flinch either.

"They're not just watching." She said. "They're listening."

Lucas stood nearby, arms folded, staring down at the feed Sophia was building. Every Share. Every mention. Every poisoned comment.

By midday, the split was clear. Half the world stood behind her. Women posting their own stories, survivors sharing screenshots of unreported abuse. Even a few high-profile influences using their platforms to say: *This is what bravery looks like.*

But the other half?

The backlash came like a virus.

Think pieces titled **"When Victimhood Becomes a Brand."** and **"Kink, Consent and the Collapse of Personal Responsibility."**

One YouTuber, a smug man with half a million followers, called her video "an Oscar-worthy audition for sympathy."

Someone tweeted a split image of her statement and the leaked footage: "Make it make sense."

And then came the bots. The trolls. The anonymous messages in her inbox calling her a liar, a whore, a manipulative little sub who regretted getting caught on camera.

Sophia's laptop dinged again. She went pale.

Lucas looked up sharply. "What?"

She turned the screen toward him.

Ethan Walker's legal team releases new statement: *"We respect Ms. Monroe's right to express herself. However, it's important to acknowledge the inconsistencies in her narrative. Our client maintains his innocence and remains hopeful the court will grant his appeal, particularly in light of this new public performance."*

"Performance," Amelia repeated, her voice flat. "Of course."

Lucas walked across the room. He crouched in front of her, his hands on her knees. "They're reaching. That's desperation."

"It's working," she said. "There are people who believe him. People who *want* to believe him."

"They want the narrative that protects them from having to look inward," Sophia added.

"You're not responsible for that."

Amelia didn't answer right away. She was watching the screen. Her face on repeat. Her voice. Her truth. And all round it, the world twisting it.

* * *

Sophia had gone home. The strategist had postponed the rest of the week's media schedule. They needed to regroup. Let the video breathe and figure out their next move.

Lucas moved like a shadow through the kitchen, setting out two glasses and opening a bottle of whisky he rarely touched.

He poured hers first, then his. She took it silently.

"Do you think I did the right thing?" she asked.

He looked at her. There was something unreadable in his expression.

"I think you did the *brave* thing," he said.

"Not the same."

"No," he admitted. "But sometimes the brave thing isn't the safe thing and that's the point."

She looked down at the glass in her hands. "I thought I'd feel….free."

"You will. But not yet."

They sat together in the growing dark, the city flickering through the windows like a distant fire.

"He doesn't have to touch me to reach me, does he?"

"No," he said. His jaw tightening. "But that doesn't mean he gets to keep reaching."

His tone was soft but the words cut like steel.

Seventeen

Chapter 17

It arrived just after midnight.

A soft chime from the elevator. One meant only for deliveries or staff access.

Lucas was up instantly. "Stay here," he said, already moving toward the door.

Amelia rose too, barefoot and heart thudding.

He opened the elevator bay to find a simple manila envelope lying on the floor.

No markings.

No courier. Nothing, just left.

He brought it inside and laid it on the kitchen island and opened it.

Inside: a folded piece of paper and a printed receipt.

The receipt was from a hotel.

The hotel.

The one where the footage was taken. The note, scrawled in

neat block letters:

You wanted the world to see the truth. Now you're going to live in it.

Amelia backed away slowly. Lucas didn't move, not at first. He read the note once and then again. Then slowly and methodically he picked up the glass of whisky he hadn't touched and shattered it against the marble countertop.

Glass splintered in every direction. Whisky pooled over the paper like spilled blood. Amelia didn't flinch. She just stared at him. Lucas braced both hands on the counter, his head looking down. Shoulders tense.

"I let him get this close," he said finally.

"You didn't…"

"I *did.*" He looked at her, eyes wild now. "I swore I'd never let anyone close enough to touch someone I loved again. That was the whole fucking point of all this."

Amelia stepped closer.

"This isn't about control," she said. "Not anymore."

He looked at her like she'd opened something in him he hadn't meant to reveal.

"I grew up in a house where I couldn't control anything. Not the yelling. Not the drinking. Not the fists. I used to hide in the fucking closet with a kitchen knife and think maybe if I stabbed him while he slept, we'd both be free."

The silence between them was deafening.

"I didn't," he added. "But I wanted to, every single night."

Amelia reached for him. "You became a protector," she whispered. "Because no one protected you."

He nodded once. The weight of it still pressed against his

throat. His jaw worked, teeth clenched so hard a muscle ticked in his cheek.

"I hate that part of me," he said, his voice rough. "The boy who wanted blood. The man who still does." His gaze flickered to her, his eyes dark and tortured. "You think I'm a protector? Some nights I wonder if I'm just a monster who learned to channel it."

She touched his face. Gentle and anchoring. "I don't need a hero, Lucas. I need you. The man who held me when I broke. The man who lets me kneel without falling."

His eyes shut, the lines of his face softening under her hand. For a moment he looked almost boyish, almost undone. Then his jaw tightened again, like the past still had its claws in him. His gaze dropped to the envelope on the table. The weight of everything it contained pressed between them like a third body.

Lucas reached for it, fingers steady this time. He didn't look at her when he stood, didn't look as he crossed the room. He only looked at the fireplace. The flames caught quick, curling the paper and devouring secrets that had poisoned them long enough.

Amelia slid her hand into his. Silent and certain. Watching the past burn down to ash at last.

Lucas hadn't spoken since. He just swept the shards into a pan, wrapped his bleeding hand in gauze and vanished into his office like a man barricading himself behind walls.

The penthouse was silent, but it wasn't at peace. It was a wound that stitched tight, throbbing under the surface.

Amelia curled into the couch, his sweater heavy on her shoulders and the scent of him clinging like smoke. The air still vibrated with the echo of his rage, sharp, hot and unfinished. She got up slowly and headed toward the office. The door was cracked open slightly, golden light spilling into the hall.

She found him in the chair by the window.

Whisky bottle untouched, lights dimmed and one hand bandaged, the other holding his phone.

The screen glowed with a single open email.

To: mumforever1957@gmail.com
Subject: (none)
Body:
You let him hurt me.

That was all. Unsent.

Lucas didn't look at her when she entered.

"I never wrote it down before," he said. "Didn't realise I needed to."

Amelia came to him slowly, like approaching a wounded animal that might bolt.

He set the phone down, face- up and stared out the window again.

"She used to be beautiful," he said. "I remember that. Before the drinking, before him. She smelled like lilies and laughed like movie stars. I didn't recognise her by the end."

He paused.

"She watched him hit me."

The words hung heavy in the room.

"She didn't stop him. She just told me to be quiet. Said I made him mad, that I needed to learn when to shut my mouth."

Amelia sat beside him, not touching. Just to be with him.

He exhaled. "I learned how to tell when he was going to hit

me. I got good at it. I could read his breathing, his eyes and I knew which belt he'd use by the sound of the drawer opening."

Amelia closed her eyes.

"I used to think that made me strong. But it didn't, it just made me obedient."

He turned his head to finally look at her.

"And then I met you."

Her heart fluttered.

"You didn't flinch when I raised my voice," he said. "You didn't blink when I gave you an order. You chose it. Every time and I didn't know how to handle that."

Amelia reached for his uninjured hand. The time he let her.

"I built this persona," he continued. "This calm one. The Dom. The protector. I'm always the one who knows what to do. Who keeps it all together but tonight…"

He looked away.

"I wanted to go to that prison and tear him apart. With my hands and teeth like an animal."

She didn't let go. "You're allowed to want that," she said softly. "You're allowed to be angry."

He shook his head. "It scared me. How much I wanted it, and how much of him I still have in me."

"No," she leaned in. "He hit because he was weak. You protect because you remember what it's like to be small."

He swallowed hard. Amelia got up slowly and moved in front of him and knelt.

Lucas's breath caught. It wasn't sexual or performative. It was just presence.

Her eyes met his. "You don't have to hold the weight alone."

He reached out with a trembling hand and brushed her hair

back. And in that moment, his entire body slumped forward. Not collapsed or broken. Just unclenched.

He leaned down until their foreheads touched. She was the still point in his storm.

They stayed like that for a while. No orders, no rituals. Just breath and being in the moment.

Two survivors. Two wolves holding each other in the dark.

Eighteen

Chapter 18

The sun hadn't even risen when the call came through.

Lucas was already up. He hadn't slept much, not after what he'd shared with Amelia the night before. His mind was quiet in a way it hadn't been in years, but his body was still tense, alert and ready.

He answered the first ring.

"Go."

It was Sophia. Her voice tight and controlled. "We have a problem. Ethan's just given his first interview from prison. It aired on a true crime podcast at midnight and it leaked in full by morning."

She played part of it over the phone. "I loved Amelia. Truly but she had complications. She didn't always know what she wanted. She could be volatile and erratic. That's not her fault. She's been through a lot. I think sometimes she misunderstood my intentions."

The host murmured back: *"It sounds like you were trying to help her."*

"Exactly, she needed structure. She said so herself and she said she felt safe when someone took control. It's all so sad really. How this turned into something ugly. I just wish she'd told the whole story."

Lucas listened to the entire thing in silence. Anger growing inside him. Amelia wrapped herself in one of his button-down shirts and sat beside him. Her hands were steady.

"He's escalating." She said, her voice was cold as steel.

Lucas nodded.

"He's laying the foundation for his appeal," she said. "Painting himself as the caring Dom. Rewriting history."

"He's not just trying to win in court," Lucas murmured. "He's trying to win in public too."

"I want to respond."

Sophia's voice rang out from the tablet on the coffee table. "Not yet. The team's already preparing a breakdown of his statement. Fact checking, framing and checking legal terminology. If you respond now, you feed into his story."

"I don't care," Amelia snapped. "I want to rip him apart."

Lucas looked at her. He recognised the fury in her eyes. He'd seen it in the mirror.

"I'll let you," he said softly. "But not until we know where to aim."

* * *

Later that day, another package arrived. This one was hand-delivered. A single white envelope. Security footage showed a woman dropping it off with the front desk. Hood up, face angled away from the cameras. She never spoke and she was gone in under fifteen seconds.

Inside the envelope was a USB drive and one sentence on a small white card:

Still want the world watching?

Lucas didn't let Amelia open it. He scanned it for malware. It came up clean so he opened the file himself on a secure laptop in the study. Amelia stood just behind him, hands folded tightly across her chest.

The video was silent. It showed her, curled up in a hospital bed, during an ER visit. Bruised. Eyes swollen and IV taped to her arm. A nurse walked in and gently took her vitals and wrote something down. She never looked at the camera.

Amelia gasped. "I didn't know he filmed that."

Lucas froze.

She stumbled backward, like the floor had been ripped out from under her.

"I was unconscious. I didn't know......"

Lucas stood instantly and caught her as she swayed. He held her tight.

"He recorded you like a trophy," he said. "He kept it and now he wants to use it."

Amelia buried her face into his chest. "He's trying to shame me again."

"No," Lucas replied. "He's trying to break you before sentencing. If you look unstable, untrustworthy, the judge might hesitate. It's a game of inches."

He pulled back enough to look in her eyes. "And he just played his last card."

She shook her head. "You don't know that."

"I know him." His voice pure fire now. "I was him. Before I learned to cage it. I know exactly how men like that think and he's losing control. That's why he's getting sloppy."

Amelia's lip trembled but her voice was sure. "Then let's make sure the next card is ours."

That night, the lights in the penthouse stayed off. Lucas stood near the windows, back lit by the city glow, watching the streets like a general before battle.

Amelia sat behind him on the couch. Her laptop open. Drafting a follow-up statement.

Lucas turned slowly. "You're winning."

She looked up. "Am I?"

"Yes."

"Then why does it feel like I'm still bleeding?"

He walked to her and sat beside her. Laid his hand on her thigh.

"Because survival isn't victory. Not yet."

She looked at him. "So what is it?"

He leaned in and whispered. "Justice." He didn't say anything else. He didn't have to.

Because the next step wasn't whispered in bedrooms or written in private journals. It was public and visible.

And it began tonight. The event for survivors. A charity gala, hosted at the downtown museum. Filled with people in black suits and dark lipstick, flashing cameras and champagne.

Amelia stood at the edge of the crowd, eyes steady, chin lifted and arms bare beneath the tailored black dress Sophia had helped her choose. Nothing flashy, nothing sexual. Just elegance turned into armour.

Lucas stood beside her in a black suit, no tie. He hadn't taken his eyes off her since they left the penthouse.

"You don't have to speak tonight," he said softly. "You've already said more than enough."

She turned to him. "No, I haven't."

There was no podium. No grand introduction. Just a moment of silence and then Amelia stepped forward. Onto a raised platform near the art exhibit. People turned and the room went quiet.

"My name is Amelia Monroe."

Every camera in the room turned.

"I've been called dramatic. A liar. A woman who uses her trauma for attention. I've been called things I won't repeat here. You've probably read them."

Her voice didn't shake. "I'm also a survivor of domestic abuse. Of rape and of psychological control. I've seen what shame can do to a person. I've lived with it. Slept beside it for year."

A few people bowed their heads. Others froze.

"I'm not here to relive that story. I'm here to reclaim it. Consent isn't a loophole. Submission is not silence. Kink is not a shield for violence and being vulnerable with someone should never be an excuse for them to destroy you."

Lucas watched her from the side of the crowd. He didn't move or speak. He just witnessed her beauty and strength. Amelia was no longer rising from the ashes. She was the fire now. She ended her speech with a single line.

"I'm not afraid of being seen anymore."

Then she stepped down. People clapped and some even

cried.

But none of that mattered. What mattered was the look she gave Lucas across the room. Not needing his approval just meeting his gaze. As his equal.

They found each other again near the exit.

He didn't say a word, just pulled her into him and pressed his lips to her temple. She melted for half and second and then whispered. "What do you see when you look at me?"

He leaned back to meet her eyes.

"I see the storm that's made for me."

Nineteen

Chapter 19

The rain hadn't stopped in days.

It ran down the floor-to-ceiling windows like veins in glass, threading the penthouse in grey light and quiet noise. Lucas stood at the far end of the rooftop terrace, shirtless beneath his open coat, his bare feet on the wet stone. The door behind him was open, cold wind threading through the space like a whisper that didn't belong.

Amelia found him like that. Still bare and his mind a million miles away. She didn't speak, not right away. Just watched the tension in his shoulders. The way his hands curled into fists and relaxed again, over and over.

When she stepped out, he didn't flinch. But his body stilled in a different way.

"I thought you'd still be asleep," he said without turning.

"I woke up cold."

He was silent a moment longer then, "I can't breathe when

I'm sleeping anymore."

She moved to stand beside him, close but not touching.

"Is it me?" She asked.

"No," he exhaled. "It's everything else."

She didn't press. She let him stand there, bones locked and silence thick.

Then he spoke again. "I used to dream about him."

Her breath hitched. "Your mother's boyfriend?"

Lucas nodded. "Not the violence, just the feeling. The waiting. The knowing. That heavy sick knowing that something was going to happen and I couldn't stop it. Couldn't fight it. I just had to take it."

She watched his hands, his knuckles were white.

"You built yourself out of that," she said softly.

"I built myself into something no one could control." He turned to her now, finally. His eyes were dark and unreadable. "And then I met you. And you asked me to control you."

Amelia's heartbeat flickered.

"I asked because I trusted you."

"I know. That's what makes it worse." His voice broke. "What if I break it? What if I become…. him.?"

She reached out and touched his chest. "You're not him, Lucas."

"You don't know what I'm capable of."

"I do." She stepped closer. "You're capable of precision. Of patience. Of dominance without destruction. I've *seen* you."

His chest rose and fell faster now. Like he was holding something in.

"I want to hurt," he whispered. "Not you. *Me*. I want to hurt so I can feel something other than this *rage.*"

Amelia's fingers tightened over his chest.

"Then give it to me."

He blinked. "What?"

She looked up at him, eyes clear.

"Give me your control. Not for punishment. For *pleasure.* For pain. For power. For *us.*"

He stared at her, chest rising like he couldn't quite breathe.

She kept going. "I want you to tie me up. I want you to scare me, in the right way. I want to feel powerless with you, not because I'm weak but because I trust you to give it back."

"Amelia…"

"*Take me.* Not gently. Not carefully. Take me like I'm your tether. Your edge. Your *cure.*"

His hand snapped out and gripped her wrist. Not painfully but tight and real.

"Do you know what you're asking?"

"Yes."

He stepped into her. "Then say it."

"I want you to dominate me tonight. Not softness. No training wheels. I want fear. I want tears. I want to *surrender so fully I forget how to breathe.*"

He growled low in his throat.

His free hand tangled in her hair and he pulled her head back just enough to meet her eyes.

"I will break you."

"No," she whispered. "You'll build me."

A pause, then he kissed her, hard and brutal. Then pulled away.

"You have until sundown," he said. "To prepare. To stretch. To kneel."

He released her. "And when I walk into that room, you are not longer my lover."

She shivered. "Who am I?"

His voice dropped like a guillotine. "You are my *object of worship and destruction*. And you will feel *everything*."

* * *

The bedroom had been transformed. Candles burned low across every surface. The mirror had been pulled from the closet and leaned against the wall at the foot of the bed. Wide, full-length, angled just enough to catch everything.

Amelia knelt on the soft rug, completely bare.

Her knees rested on the black velvet cushion, thighs spread just enough to be open but not obscene. Hands rested palm-down on her thighs. Her hair was bound in a loose braid down her back. Her body was trembling but it wasn't from fear. It was anticipation. The silk blindfold rested beside her and the rope was coiled at her feet.

Lucas stood in the doorway like a storm waiting to touch down.

He was dressed in black. His shirt sleeves rolled to the elbows, chest rising slow and deep with every breath. His eyes were not soft. They were black glass.

She didn't look up and he didn't speak. The silence stretched between them.

His gaze locked on hers. "Colour?"

Her pulse jumped. "Green, Sir."

"Safe word?" His voice low and testing like he was daring her to say it.

"Lavender."

His hand hovered near her throat, not touching yet. "And if I put pressure here?"

She swallowed hard. "Two taps to stop or 'lavender' out loud."

"You asked for this," he said." You wanted to the dark."

"I still do."

"Then give me your fear."

Her breath caught. "Yes, Sir."

"Tonight, you don't speak unless I demand it. You don't ask questions. You don't beg. You endure."

"Yes, Sir."

Lucas picked up the rope. It was thick and heavy. He began with her arms, slow and methodical. Wrapping them behind her back, crossing wrists, knotting with precision. The pressure grew but not unbearable.

Each pass of rope drew her tighter into herself.

"Look at the mirror," he said, his voice low.

She obeyed.

"You're going to watch everything I do to you."

She whimpered.

He looped the rope around her chest now, framing her breasts. Tugging tight so that every breath pushed her against the knots. Her nipples pebbled under the air. He moved behind her, tied the final knot against the small of her back and exhaled against her ear.

"You look like a painting." He murmured. "A ruin I want to worship and desecrate in equal measure."

Her eyes fluttered shut, a broken moan slipping past her lips. Shame and heat collided in her chest. The ropes held her steady, but inside she was unravelling.

"Silence," he growled, voice rough as the ropes biting into

her skin. "No pleasure until I say."

Her breath hitched. She bit her lip hard enough to taste copper, forcing herself to hold it in, every nerve screaming for release.

Lucas reached for the blindfold and slid it over her eyes. "Now you're mine."

She was nothing but skin and sound now. Bound and blindfolded. Her breathing coming in ragged.

Lucas circled her like a slow orbit, each step deliberate. His feet against the hardwood, the faint brush of air as he moved past her. She felt him, not just physically but energetically.

"I wonder," he murmured," how long you'll last tonight."

She swallowed hard.

He was behind her again, then suddenly in front. She felt the warmth of his body even though he wasn't touching her.

"I haven't even started yet," he whispered. "And you're already shaking and ready."

A whimper escaped her lips.

His hand snapped into her hair, not to hurt but to anchor. He yanked her head back.

"No sound."

She gasped and he released her.

Her knees wobbled and then the first touch came. Not a hand.

A blade.

Cool metal at her throat. Not sharp. A dull edge of a small ceremonial knife, cold and unforgiving.

She froze.

Lucas's voice slid behind her ear like a silk noose.

"I could cut the rope. Or your skin. Or your fear. Tell me,

Amelia," His lips brushed her temple. "What are you hoping I'll do?"

Her lips trembled.

She didn't answer.

Good.

He didn't want her words. He wanted her body to speak.

He dragged the blunt blade down her chest, slow and teasing. Between her breasts. Across her ribs. The metal kissed her navel, then lifted away.

She moaned before she could stop herself.

He was behind her in an instant, hand in her braid. Tugging her head back again.

"I said no sound."

Tears welled under the blindfold.

He knelt beside her now. His breath against her ear.

He grabbed her by the throat, firm and possessive.

He counted.

"One. Two. Three. Four."

Then he released.

She gasped, air flooding her lungs.

He kissed her neck, sweet and tender.

"Do you trust me?" He asked.

"Yes, Sir."

"Then suffer for me."

He moved in front of her again. This time he touched her. One finger sliding between her thighs.

She was soaking.

"You ache," he whispered. "You want to fall apart."

She nodded, trembling.

"But you don't get to come until I say. You don't even get to want it."

"Yes, sir." She said her tongue trailing her lips.

Lucas stood. He stepped behind her.

Then the **crop.**

The sound came before the pain.

A crack across the back of her thigh. Sharp and searing.

She gasped, nearly tipping forward.

Another. Then another.

He didn't speak, he just broke her open with rhythm and restraint.

And then he stopped.

Silence. Her body throbbing. He knelt before her again.

"Colour?"

"G….green." She sobbed.

"Good girl." He praised as he removed the blindfold. Light flooded back. Her reflection was a ruin in beauty. Flushed cheeks, tear streaks, ropes biting into her soft skin and her thighs trembling, her pussy slick and swollen.

He slid his fingers between her legs, thrusting deep. She cried out, her body arching.

"Come for me."

She shattered with a scream that was half a prayer and half surrender.

"Yes, yes yes." she chanted. Her orgasm ripped through her like wildfire, leaving her gasping and her pussy clenching around his fingers.

He didn't rush. He lowered her gently to the rug, untying her wrists carefully. Her arms fell limp.

"Look at me," he said.

Her eyes fluttered open. He stripped his shirt off, muscles taut with restrained need. His cock was thick and dripping pre-cum. He knelt between her thighs, spreading her wide.

"Say it," he commanded.

"I'm yours," she gasped.

He entered her in one slow, devastating thrust. Her body stretched to take him, slick and aching. He moved deliberately at first, deep and grounding. His eyes locked onto hers. Each thrust forced a broken moan from her lips.

Lucas groaned, his body shuddering as he spilled into her, his forehead pressed to hers as they shook together.

They collapsed, their bodies slick with sweat. He rolled off her, pulling her into his arms. She snuggled against him, her body still trembling from the aftershocks of her orgasm.

"That was incredible," she whispered.

He smiled, his hand stroking her hair. "You were incredible."

They stayed like that for a long time, no words just warmth. Then he moved gently and she whimpered at the sound of his absence. He kissed her temple. "Bath. You don't have to walk. I've got you."

He carried her to the master bathroom. The tub was steaming. Rose oil shimmered on the surface.

Lucas stepped into the water with her still in his arms.

He sat first, then pulled her into his lap, cradling her against his chest as the water surrounded them.

Amelia exhaled like she was shedding an entire lifetime.

He reached for the washcloth, dipped it and wrung it out and began cleaning her. Starting with the shoulders, her collarbone. The dried salt of tears. Faint bruises already blooming along her thighs.

He didn't speak. He just washed like she was a temple. By

the time he reached her hands, still red from the rope, she was crying again. Quiet but steady.

Lucas kissed each finger. "You're not crying because you're hurt." He said softly.

"No," she whispered. "I'm crying because I've never felt more whole."

He closed his eyes and let her lean into him again.

"Let me take care of you," she said.

He stilled. "What?"

"Let me touch you. You give me everything, let me give something back."

She turned in the water, slowly straddling his lap. Her fingers reached for the edge of his jaw. She kissed his chest and then thin white scar under his collarbone.

Lucas trembled.

"You don't have to be strong for me anymore," she whispered. "You can just be."

His hands slid to her waist and held her tight.

"I don't know how," he admitted.

"You don't have to." She kissed his throat, his shoulder and his scarred knuckles.

For the first time, he let himself be loved without performance. Without dominance.

When they climbed out of the bath, she dried him first. Wrapped him in a towel and led him back to bed. Not for sex or power just for the quiet of being together. And that quiet was healing.

Twenty

Chapter 20

The room was quiet when Amelia walked in.

It smelled like coffee and cleaning spray. The room had beige walls and folding chairs were out for people to sit on. A box of tissues in the centre.

She was the last to arrive.

"Take any seat," the facilitator said gently.

Amelia slid into a chair near the back. Lucas had offered to wait outside but she'd asked him not to come at all. This wasn't for him. This was for her.

Around the circle were seven women and one man. All different ages, all with their own scars.

"I'm Jade," said the facilitator, a clipboard resting on her knees. "Tonight's theme is control. When it was taken and how we are learning to take it back."

No one spoke for a moment.

Then a woman with salt and pepper curls cleared her throat.

"I didn't leave. Not for twenty years. You want to know why?"

No one answered. They just let her share what she needed to.

"Because I had kids. Because he never hit me. Because he was good in public and I thought maybe it wasn't that bad."

The girl beside her, barely more then a teenager bit her lip. "Mine only lasted six months. But he posted photos after I broke up with him. Said I like it rough, that I begged."

Amelia looked down at her hands.

Another woman leaned forward. "Can I say something kind of unpopular?"

The room quieted.

"I don't want to reclaim sex," she said. "I don't want to be touched again. Everyone keeps talking about empowerment through pleasure and that's great but I just want to feel nothing sometimes. And that should be okay too."

Amelia felt something crack open inside her.

"I saw your video," the young girl whispered, her eyes on Amelia now. "The leaked one and then the one where you spoke after."

Amelia froze.

"I didn't believe you at first," she said. "Because it looked like submission. Like the stuff I've seen online."

Amelia's stomach twisted.

"But then you explained the difference," the girl added. "How consent can't be taken even if it starts with a 'yes'. And I realised I said yes to. Once, just once and he used it against me."

Amelia lifted her eyes. "I used to think if I said yes once, I had to take everything after that. Even the things I never agreed to because I'd already given him the power."

Jade nodded slowly. "And now?"

Amelia's voice was quiet but clear. "Now I'm learning power isn't permanent. It's a loan and you can take it back anytime."

The room exhaled. Some nodded and some cried.

The girl across from her smiled through tears. "Good."

Twenty-One

Chapter 21

The envelope was cream-coloured. Government issued.

Lucas recognised it the moment the concierge brought it up. Sealed. Stamped and official.

Amelia was on the couch, reading through the early press surrounding the sentencing hearing. The glow from her tablet lit her face in soft light.

She looked up when she heard the elevator and she knew instantly something was wrong.

Lucas handed her the envelope in silence. She opened it without flinching.

He watched her read, her eyes moved once, then twice and she slowly closed it.

"I thought he might try," she said.

Lucas's jaw ticked. "What does it say?"

She passed it to him.

To Ms. Monroe.

In accordance with State Statute 487.2-B regarding victim-defendant dialogue prior to sentencing, the incarcerated party, Ethan Walker, has formally requested a voluntary in-person meeting. This request does not constitute a court order and may be declined without legal consequence.

If you choose to accept, a supervised, recorded meeting will be arranged within the next five business days at the Jefferson County Correctional Facility. Please respond via counsel or direct contact within 48 hours.

Lucas's hand shook. "You're not going," he said aloud.

Amelia didn't speak.

He looked over at her. "You're not going."

She still didn't answer and he could see he thinking about it.

"Amelia!" His voice darkened. Not a command. A plea. "This is bait."

"I know."

"He wants to manipulate you."

"I know Lucas."

"He wants to see if he still lives under your skin."

She looked at him then and that look said everything. A woman who'd already made peace with the nightmare and was now walking back into it with her chin high and her spine straight.

"I'm going."

Lucas sat down hard across from her. "No."

"Yes."

His hands curled into fists. "You don't need this, closure is just a myth."

"I'm not doing this for closure." She leaned forward. "I'm

doing it for clarity. I want to see what he looks like now. Not in my head, not in court but there. Behind those bars and in chains. With no power left to steal."

Lucas stared at her but she didn't blink. She was determined.

"I want to remember," she said quietly. "That I walked out and he didn't."

Lucas looked down at the paper again, his voice dropped low. "What if he says something that rips you open?"

"Then you'll be there to hold me." she said reaching for his hand.

"And if I can't stay still?" he asked. "If I lose it?"

"You won't."

"You don't know that Amelia."

"I know you love me," she said. "And I trust you."

Lucas leaned back like her words had knocked the wind out of him.

"You trust me more than I trust myself."

She nodded. "Yes I do."

He ran a hand over his face.

"You'll be watched. Guarded. I can't touch him. You understand that?"

"I don't need you to touch him Lucas," she whispered. "I just need you with me."

He looked at her for a long time, then stood and walked toward the window.

"You'll wear the collar," he said.

A pause then she nodded. "Yes, sir."

His voice cracked around the words. "Then we'll go."

* * *

The prison was colder then it needed to be. Fluorescent lights buzzed above their heads. The walls were a shade of beige that had long since given up on being anything else. Time didn't pass here. It stalled. Stuck in the hum of locked doors and the shuffle of chained men behind bars.

Lucas walked beside Amelia, his hand resting at the small of her back. Protective. Possessive and grounded.

She wore black. A simple blouse, sleeves rolled to her elbows. No jewellery, no makeup. Her collar rested snugly at her throat, a thin line of matte leather and steel.

A single statement. I belong to no one but myself and the man I choose.

The guard led them into a small meeting room. Pale walls, a bolted table and two chairs on either side. A camera above the door. A clock that ticked too loudly. Lucas scanned the space like a soldier checking for exits and danger.

Amelia sat first.

Lucas remained standing.

Then the door opened and Ethan Walker walked in.

His hands were cuffed and his ankles shackled. His prison jumpsuit was clean, pressed, the sleeves rolled like he thought it made him look casual. His hair was shorter now but his smile?

Still there. That same, cold smile.

He looked at Amelia first.

Then at Lucas.

"Wow," he said. "Didn't expect an audience."

Lucas didn't speak. His jaw clenched once.

Ethan sat.

"Thanks for coming," he said to Amelia. "I wasn't sure you would. I figured you might be still too…" He gestured vaguely toward her. "Fragile."

Amelia tilted her head. "I'm not."

Ethan chuckled. "So I see. Leather and everything. Bold choice for a prison visit."

Lucas stepped forward slightly.

Amelia raised a hand without looking. "Don't," she said softly. "He wants a reaction."

Ethan leaned back. "So he listens to you now. That's new."

Lucas didn't move. Didn't speak.

But his eyes never left Ethan.

"You requested this," Amelia said. "So talk."

Ethan shrugged. "I don't have a speech. Just some thoughts."

"Spare me the monologue."

That wiped the smile from his face, just for a second.

But it returned thinner and more venomous.

"I just miss the way things were," he said. "Before all the mess. Before you decided what we had was abuse."

Amelia didn't blink. "You mean before I stopped surviving and started remembering."

"Semantics," Ethan said.

"No," she replied. "Consent."

His smile faltered.

"You know," he said, voice lower now. "There were times I thought you wanted it rough. You never said stop."

"I was dissociating," she said. "And when I did say no, you didn't listen."

He shrugged. "I remember things differently."

"That's because you're a liar." Lucas said quiet and dangerous.

Ethan looked at him now. "Is that what she told you? That I was a monster?"

Lucas didn't answer. He didn't have to.

Ethan leaned forward, smile gone now and his tone shifting.

"I've seen your file, you know. Lucas Cross. I know about your little incident when you were seventeen. The guy you put in the hospital. How long did you spend in juvie? Two years?"

Lucas's hands curled into fists.

Amelia's voice cut through the air. "Enough."

She turned fully toward Ethan. "You wanted to see me. So see me. Look at the woman you tried to erase."

He did, and something shifted in his face.

Not recognition, not regret but fear. It was just a flicker but it was enough for her to notice.

"I don't care if they lock you up for five years or fifty." Amelia said. "Because what you lost isn't time. It's me."

"You'll always think of me," Ethan said. "When he touches you. When he calls you 'good girl'. You'll wonder if you're just repeating the same cycle. If you're still the same broken little thing who let me ruin her."

Lucas moved just a step. But the sound of his boot on the concrete echoed like thunder and made Ethan Flinch slightly.

Amelia smiled. "No," she said. "Because you didn't ruin me. You revealed me."

He frowned.

She stood.

"You're not a ghost. You're not a scar." She leaned down slightly, voice low and calm.

"You're dust."

Then she turned and Lucas followed. They didn't look back. Not once. Not on the walk out of the prison. Not in the garage where their driver waited with the engine running. Lucas kept one hand on the small of Amelia's back, but it wasn't possessive this time.

It was a lifeline.

Like if he let go, he'd drown.

They climbed into the back seat and the doors shut. Amelia reached for his hand. He didn't take it. He was staring straight ahead, jaw clenched, his breath shallow like he was holding in a scream that had no exit.

She watched him for a moment. "Talk to me," she said softly.

Nothing.

"I need you to come back now."

His jaw twitched.

Then he said, flat and cold. "He sounded like my mother."

Amelia blinked.

Lucas kept staring ahead. "The way he twisted things. Like what happened was mutual. Like pain is something people ask for."

She said nothing. Just sat there listening.

"I wanted to kill him," he said quieter now. "I mean that. I wanted to reach across that table and crush his throat until I watched the light leave his fucking eyes."

"Lucas…"

"I wanted it. And for one second, I thought about doing it. With you right there."

He finally turned to her. His eyes shattered.

"You trusted me and all I could think about was tearing a man apart.

He laughed, bitter and hollow.

"Some Dom I am."

She leaned in. "You didn't move. You stayed with me."

"I didn't stay with you," he snapped. "I stayed in control because that's all I've ever had."

Amelia reached for him again, this time laying her hand on his knee.

"You're not what he made of you either," she said.

But he shook his head.

"You don't get it," he said, his breathing picking up. "I've built my whole life around being the safe one. The calm one. The man who never snaps. But inside me? It's always waiting. That boy with a bloody mouth and broken ribs. The one who waited for the door to open and prayed it wouldn't be his turn."

He turned to her fully now.

"I've learned to be quiet. I learned to take it. Until one day I didn't and I hurt someone. Bad."

Amelia's heart cracked. He'd never told her this. No one had ever seen this version of him.

"I put him in the hospital," he said. "Seventeen years old. Broken beer bottle and I don't even remember doing it. Just the blood and the noise. The way my mother screamed when they took me away."

Amelia slipped to the floor of the car, knelt between his legs and rested her hands on his thighs.

His eyes widened.

"Don't kneel for me now," he rasped. "Not when I …."

"I'm not kneeling for you." She said. "I'm kneeling with you."

And in that moment the dam broke. He covered his face with both hands and his body shook as sobs fell.

She crawled into his lap and held him. Cradled him like a man who had never been held the right way. His arms locked around her, face pressed into her shoulder. Amelia stroked his hair and whispered, "You're allowed to break. You're allowed to bleed. Because I will still be here when you come back together."

Twenty-Two

Chapter 22

The drive was long. Miles of winding forest road, the canopy so thick in places it turned midday into twilight. No signs. No gates. No markers. Just the hum of tires on pavement and the deep silence between them. It wasn't an awkward silence but the kind that thrummed with promise.

Amelia had stopped asking where they were going hours ago. Lucas had simply placed his hand over hers in the centre console and said, "Where we go next, no one else gets to follow."

When the car finally pulled through a nearly invisible break in the trees, the estate revealed itself like a secret finally ready to be shared.

It wasn't ostentatious.

It was ancient. Stone walls. Tall arched windows. Ivy crawling along the side like nature was trying to reclaim it. There was beauty in it but also shadow. A weight. Like this place had seen things.

Lucas stepped out of the car first, walked around and opened the door for her.

She slid out, boots crunching on gravel.

The air was colder here.

"Where are we?" She asked.

He didn't answer with words.

He took her hand, laced his fingers with hers and led her to the front doors.

Inside was quiet luxury. Polished wood floors. Iron sconces. Dark velvet curtains that swallowed the light. A fireplace already burning in the main hall. The air smelled like sandalwood, stone and something warmer.

Amelia turned slowly in place.

"This place…" she breathed.

"No one has ever been here," Lucas said behind her. "Not with me."

She turned.

"You sometimes live here?"

"No," he said. "I retreat here. It's not where I go to exist. It's where I go to feel."

Her breath caught as he stepped closer.

"There are things I've only ever done in theory. Fantasies. Rituals I've written and rewritten in my head."

She looked into his eyes. "And you bought me here to do them?"

"I bought you here because I want to share them." He touched her face. "You don't just take what I give, Amelia. You pull it from me. Every dark thought. Every unspoken command. Every part I thought I'd buried.

She pressed her body against his now, slow and deliberate.

"Then give me everything."

His breath hitched. "Not tonight," he said, his voice low and dominant, "Tonight, you'll ask for it."

She arched a brow. "You're assuming I'll beg."

He smiled. Dark and slow.

"You'll weep."

* * *

Later that evening, after she'd showered and changed into the silk robe laid out on the bed. A gift clearly chosen by him. They met in the east wing.

The door was matte black. The handle gold. She opened it without hesitation and stepping inside a room built for worship.

Tall mirrors framed all four walls. Chains and cuffs anchored into the floorboards. A padded bench. A Saint Andrew's cross and a narrow leather table with silk straps at the head and foot.

Lucas stood by the far wall, rope coiled in one hand and a riding crop in the other.

She stopped in the doorway.

Lucas pointed to the floor in front of him. "Kneel."

She moved without hesitation. The robe slid off her shoulders as she lowered herself. He dropped the rope and tossed the crop. He reached for her face.

"I don't want silence tonight," he murmured. "I want your moans, your tears and your shamelessness. "

"Yes, Sir."

He unbuttoned his shirt as he spoke. "You'll be restrained, blindfolded, denied and used.

She licked her lips. "Good."

136

He smirked. Then yanked her up by her hair and slammed his mouth into hers.

It wasn't a kiss. It was claiming. He devoured her, tongue, teeth, breath. One hand fisted in her hair, the other sliding between her thighs.

She gasped into his mouth.

"So wet already," he growled. "You've missed this. You've missed being ruined."

She moaned and he spun her around and bent her over the padded bench. He yanked her hands behind her back and snapped the cuffs closed. She was helpless in seconds.

"Colour?" he asked, already palming her ass.

"Green,' She gasped. He grinned against her neck and the first strike came hard and fast.

The crop, hitting the back of her thighs.

She cried out, spine arching. Again and again. Five strokes in and she was panting.

Lucas knelt behind her. Ran his tongue up the inside of her pussy.

"Beg." He commanded.

She whimpered.

"Louder." He said as he spanked her again.

"Please."

He didn't touch her.

"Say what you want."

"I want you to fuck me," she gasped.

He stood and undid his belt, pushing his pants down. And then he was inside her , one thrust brutal and perfect.

She screamed.

He fucked her hard, deep and relentless. Each thrust punctuated by a growl, a command, a filthy promise.

"You're mine."

"Take it."

"Every inch."

"You were made for this."

"Made for me."

She came. Her orgasm tearing through her. Then he pulled out, flipped her onto her back and crawled over her, kissing her throat, her collarbone and her mouth.

"You still with me?" he asked.

Her eyes met his.

"Always." She smiled and whispered. "But you haven't broken me yet."

His grin was savage.

Amelia's wrists were bound in front of her now, tight, elegant rope work framed her arms like sculpture. Her ankles were cuffed and pulled wide to the corners of the padded leather table. Her back arched naturally, thighs trembling and her eyes now covered by the blindfold. Her mouth parted in breathless need.

Lucas stood above her, he traced the rope with his fingers.

"You wanted dark." He murmured.

She nodded, lips barely able to form sound. "Yes, Sir."

"You want to be taken."

"I want to be destroyed."

He leaned in, voice a growl at her ear.

"Then I'll rebuild you from ash."

He reached between her thighs, fingers dragging slowly through her wet pussy. She shivered.

"Already wrecked," he said admiring her. "You come so beautifully for me."

He didn't enter her, he just teased. Circling her clit with the pad of his thumb. Pressing only when she whimpered backing off when she started to pant.

"Lucas….."

He gripped her throat, firm but safe, silencing her.

"You don't speak unless I give you permission."

Her entire body pulsed.

"Understood?"

"Yes, Sir."

He released her.

Then came the clamps. He twisted her nipples, pinched them gently then clipped them with metal lined in velvet. She gasped, back arching and rope biting into her thighs as her breath quickened.

"You'll thank me," he said.

"I already do."

Lucas picked up the crop again. Starting at her inner thigh. Crack.

She moaned.

Then her stomach.

Crack.

Then across her breasts, careful, precise and landing between the clamps.

Crack.

She sobbed and then he touched her.

Two fingers sliding inside her, slow and deep, curling just right.

She started to shake.

"Don't come." he warned.

She tried. God she tried. But when he pulled the clamps off and thrust back inside her in one brutal move, she shattered.

Screaming and clenching around him. Soaking the table. He didn't stop.

He fucked her through it. Grinding into her, one hand on her throat, the other gripping the rope bound wrists as she came again and again. Her sobs turning into begging.

"Please…Sir….I can't…"

"Yes." He growled. "You can."

He pulled out and stroked himself. Fast and hard. His eyes locked on her trembling, ruined body.

"Open your mouth."

She obeyed, eyes wide behind the blindfold.

He came with a groan that sounded like pain and prayer. Spilling across her tongue, her lips and her chest. Marking her.

"Don't swallow."

He undid her blindfold, slow.

She looked up at him, wrecked and radiant.

"Now." He said.

She swallowed.

He kissed her, slow and deep. Then released her wrists and uncuffed her ankles.

He lifted her like she weighed nothing and carried her to a fur lined chaise by the fire. Sat with her in his lap, her thighs straddling his hips as her head tucked under his chin.

The silence was thick with heat and something holy.

She was floating and he was trembling. And then he said it low, barely more than a breath. "I don't want to just protect you, Amelia. I want to belong to you."

She lifted her head slowly to meet his gaze.

"Say it again."

He reached up and took her hand, placing it over his heart. "I want to belong to you," he whispered. "Not as a game. Not as play. As truth."

Her lips parted.

"You've always owned me," she said. "And I don't want to belong to anyone else."

He smiled but it was wounded. "I've never belonged to anyone who didn't want to hurt me eventually."

Amelia leaned in, kissed the scar beneath his eye. Then the one near his ribs and whispered into his mouth, "Then let me be the first."

Lucas didn't answer, at least not with words. He stood slowly, his hands steady now and brushed her hair back.

"Stay here,"he said, voice low and warm. "I'll run you a bath."

Amelia nodded, breath caught between her ribs.

He disappeared into the bathroom.

She heard the water running. The soft clink of a candle being lit. A drawer opening and the low rustle of fabric as he pulled the towels from the shelf. Then the scent hit her…. lavender, vanilla and a touch of something warm and earthy.

Safety.

When he returned, he didn't rush her. He just held out his hand.

She took it and he led her to the bathroom.

He helped her into the tub, guiding her down until the water cradled her completely.

Amelia sank into the warmth with a trembling breath.

Lucas knelt beside the tub. He didn't touch her yet, he just watched. Not like a man looking at something fragile. But like a man looking at something sacred.

"You did so well for me tonight," he murmured.

Her throat tightened.

"You gave me everything and now I get to give it back." He reached for the cloth, dipped it in the water and began to wash her. Starting with her arms, slow circles from shoulder to wrist. He lifted her hand and kissed each knuckle, then moved on to her collar bone, neck and chest.

Each place marked with rope, sweat or tears, he touched with care.

Amelia closed her eyes and her breath steadied.

He washed between her thighs, tender and unhurried, then guided her knees up to rest on the edge of the tub. He dried each one before they could cool.

Then he kissed her temple.

"Lean forward for me, sweetheart."

She did and he began to rinse her hair, careful not to get water in her eyes. His fingers worked through the strands like silk, slow and grounding.

"I've got you," he said. "There's nothing you have to do now. Just exist and be mine."

A tear slipped down her cheek. Not from pain but from peace. Lucas noticed and kissed it away.

The silence wrapped around them like steam, warm, thick and safe.

He dried her gently, each limb handled like a secret. Then he pulled her into his arms and carried her from the bathroom. Her head rested against his shoulder, her body boneless. Floating in the afterglow of care.

Lucas set her down on the bed and climbed in behind her. Wrapping a blanket around them and snuggled into her until she fell asleep.

Twenty-Three

Chapter 23

The night pressed against the estate like a living thing. Wind rattled the ivy on the stone walls, carrying whispers Amelia couldn't quite decipher. The fire in their room had died down to embers, painting Lucas's face in shadows and soft red light.

He had been quiet since the bath. Not distant but like a man carrying something heavy in his chest. She could feel it in the way his hands lingered on her thigh, in the silence that stretched between his breaths.

Amelia curled closer, searching his eyes. "Lucas.."

He finally looked at her, gaze sharp as glass and just as breakable.

"I want to show you something," he said softly.

Amelia looked up, eyes half lidded but steady. "What is it?" He took her hand and led her down the hallway.

It was the only locked door in the estate.

Not the playroom.

Not the weapons cabinet.

Not even the server room where Lucas monitored his private surveillance systems.

This door was old. Wood worn and the keyhole carved by hand. The hinges weren't modern but iron. The lock was brass, tarnished and Lucas wore the key on a chain around his neck.

They stood outside the door barefoot, robes loosely tied. Her hair was still damp from the bath he'd drawn for her earlier. Lucas reached for the chain slowly and held the key in his hand.

Amelia didn't move, she just waited.

Lucas stepped forward, slid the key into the lock and turned it.

The latch clicked like a gun cocking.

The door opened inward.

The room was dim and dustless.

The walls were lined with shelves, not of books but of small, careful objects. A cracked leather collar. A bundle of frayed rope, bloodstained at the ends. A series of notebooks, numbered and sealed with black wax. A single photo in a frame.

Lucas closed the door behind them.

"This is where I buried him," he said.

She turned. "The boy?"

He nodded. "The one who hid in closets. The one who took punches and told himself it was love. The one who snapped."

He crossed to the table and picked up the photo frame and held it out to her.

Amelia took it. It was blurry. Old. A boy, sixteen or

seventeen. Eyes hollow, blood down one side of his face. He was standing over a man whose face had been blurred. On the hospital gurney.

"I didn't even remember the photo existed," Lucas said. "But they used it in the court case. Printed it in the file. I kept it. Because I need to remember what I survived and what I did."

Amelia stared at the boy in the photo.

Then looked up.

"You were still a kid."

"I was a loaded weapon."

He walked to a shelf and picked up the collar.

"It was hers," he said. "My first Domme. Years later. She was older. Beautiful until she wasn't.

Amelia's breath caught.

"She used the word 'obedience' when what she meant was 'silence'. She made pain feel like something I deserved."

He dropped the collar back onto the shelf.

"I left in the middle of the night with a broken rib and a broken contract. And I swore I'd never submit again."

He looked at her now. "But sometimes," he said, voice rough. "I still ache for it. Not because I want pain but because I want to be seen. Owned. Not used but claimed."

Amelia walked to him and laid her hand on his chest.

"I don't want your control," she said. "I want you."

She pressed her forehead to his. "Let me have all of you."

He leaned in and whispered, "Then take me."

Twenty-Four

Chapter 24

The room was warm with firelight. The air between them didn't tremble with lust, it burned with worship.

Lucas stood before her naked, his chest rising slow with each breath like he was offering his body as a confession.

No chains.

No ropes.

Just choice.

And then he dropped to his knees.

Head bowed and his cock thick and hard between his legs.

"Look at me," Amelia said softly.

He lifted his eyes. They weren't full of fear, they were full of need.

"Do you understand what kneeling means?" She asked.

"Yes."

"Say it."

"It means I give everything," he said. "My control, my body, my pleasure and my release."

She stepped forward and ran her fingers through his hair. Gripping just enough to make his breath catch.

"It means you trust me to wreck you," she whispered. "And to put you back together."

"Yes."

"Do you?"

"I want you to."

She smiled, then slapped him. Not hard, just enough to cause a sting. His eyes fluttered closed and his lips parted. A soft moan escaping.

"You like that?"

He nodded.

"Good because you'll earn more."

She circled him now, like a predator stalking prey that begged to be taken. She ran her nails across his shoulder blades, down his spine and left light red trails in their wake. Making him shiver.

Then she sat on the chaise.

"Crawl." She commanded.

He obeyed. Palms flat to the floor, knees sinking into the thick carpet, cock dragging heavy between his legs as he moved toward her.

When he reached her, she opened her robe.

He leaned in and kissed the inside of her knee.

She slapped him again, firmer this time.

"Don't touch until I say."

He dropped his gaze.

"Yes, Ma'am."

The words sent heat through her, curling low and sharp.

She stood and let the robe fall. Then she pointed to the mat on the floor.

"Lie down, arms above your head and legs apart."

He obeyed.

She walked over to him and straddled his face.

His moans vibrated against her slit before he ever licked.

and when he did, fuck when he did, it was filthy. Tongue lapping, nose pressed to her clit, sucking and groaning like she was his final meal.

She gripped his sides and rode his mouth. Grinding her pussy against his tongue until she came so hard she nearly blacked out.

Then she stood and slapped his face with her wetness still slick on his lips.

"Good boy."

Lucas panted. His cock was leaking against his stomach.

"You're not allowed to come," she said. Making him whimper.

She knelt beside him, now straddling his chest and leaned in.

"What do you want?"

"You."

"Say it right."

"I want you to ride me, use me and break me."

She dragged her nails downs his chest leaving red welts. Then she reached for a set of cuffs and a silk blindfold.

He stiffened but didn't stop her.

"You trust me?" she asked again.

"Yes."

She teased his cock, sliding her soaked pussy along the length of it without letting him enter.

Again and again. Until he was straining against the cuffs, his jaw tight and gasping.

"Please." he choked.

"You think you've earned me?"

"I'll do anything."

She leaned down, dragged her tongue across his chest, then bit just below his collarbone. Hard. He groaned and she lined him up and sank down slowly. Tight and deep.

He cursed, shoulders shaking. But she didn't move. She sat there, fully impaled on his cock.

He whimpered beneath her and she smiled.

"You want to come?"

"Yes."

"Beg."

"Please, Ma'am. Please ride me. Fuck me until I forget my name."

She leaned back and rode him. Brutal, sharp and relentless.

She bounced on his cock until her thighs burned, her body slapping against his. Her moans building into screams as she used every inch of him.

And Lucas took it. "Don't stop." he gasped.

She didn't, she rode him hard and fast until she came again and again.

And then she stopped without letting him finish.

She slid off and crawled down his body. Stroking his thick length in her hand and she opened her mouth and devoured him.

Slow at first then faster. He begged to come but she slapped his hip.

"Don't come until I say."

He nodded, trembling.

She sucked him like worship, tongue twisting, mouth deep.

When he was seconds away, she stopped again. He sobbed as she crawled back up and lowered herself onto him again.

"Come." she whispered in his ear as she rode him slow and deep.

He exploded screaming her name and when it was over, when his body had stilled , spent and drenched in sweat she laid beside him.

He turned and curled into her chest. Held her like she was salvation.

"I've never given myself like that to anyone. He whispered.

She kissed his forehead and they laid there for hours.

Twenty-Five

Chapter 25

The message came encrypted. It arrived through one of Lucas's ghost servers. Channels only his most trusted digital contacts use. A simple ping on his phone. Unmarked and no subject.

He knew what that meant before he even opened it.

Something had gone wrong.

He was in the study and Amelia was upstairs, wrapped in one of his sweaters and curled up with a book. She didn't know the world was about to shift again.

Lucas clicked the link. A secure window opened. No buffering, no loading. Just the video.

And for a full three seconds he couldn't move. It was of them.

Him and Amelia. In the estate bedroom. Two nights ago.

She was naked and kneeling. He was behind her, hand tangled in her braid, whispering low things that made her shudder in his arms.

The camera didn't shake or blur. It had been set up. Fixed and hidden.

Lucas's chest locked. The timestamp was in the corner. The location data burned into the code.

His estate. His sanctuary. His fucking bed.

He didn't feel the whisky glass slip from his hand until it shattered on the floor. He just stared and something cold and angry settled in his chest.

He called his dark web security team.

"Mr. Cross." came a voice on the line. Crisp and British. "We've seen it."

"How long?"

"Fifteen minutes. It was uploaded to a closed-access onion directory. Five hundred downloads so far. Possibly more from mirrors."

"Scrub it."

"We're already working on it. But someone wants it out there. They are spreading it through encrypted clusters. The architecture is complex."

"I don't care if it's complex," Lucas said, his voice flat. "Burn it, every copy, every device that's touched it. I want IP trails. I want server smoke. I want names."

"Yes, sir."

"Find the leak."

A pause. Then the voice came back low.

"We believe the camera was embedded in the east mirror. Custom job. Infrared-sensitive. No exterior wiring."

Lucas didn't speak. Not for several seconds.

When he did, his voice was like ice.

"Kill the source."

He went upstairs to where Amelia was. She was by the window on the chaise, snuggled up and reading a book.

She looked up. Her face shifted the moment she saw his expression.

"Lucas?"

He crossed the room in three long strides and crouched in front of her. Took her face in both hands and said, "Listen to me."

She froze.

"There's something you need to see."

He pulled out his phone and pressed play. She watched the whole video and to her credit she didn't flinch.

Her lips parted, and her fingers tightened slightly around the armrest. But she didn't recoil. She didn't cry. She watched herself get used, loved and claimed. Then said softly, "That's from the bedroom."

He nodded.

"Who saw it?"

Lucas looked at her and the fury in his eyes wasn't hot, it was lethal. "Everyone."

She breathed in and then out and said the last thing he expected. "Do you still want to fuck me right now?"

He blinked. "What?"

"Because that's what this was suppose to take. That feeling." She sat up straighter, her voice calm. "That connection. That power. He wanted to shame us out of our skin."

Lucas leaned in, gripping the edge of the chaise.

"I want to end him."

"I know."

His voice dropped to a growl. "I'll burn every server, every buyer and every sick bastard who clicked 'play'. I'll do it without mercy."

She laid her hand on his chest and felt the quake beneath.

"I'm not afraid of your rage," she whispered. "I'm afraid of what happens if you bottle it again."

He gritted his teeth.

"I was supposed to protect you."

"You did." Her eyes were bright now. Fierce. "And now I'm going to protect you."

He sat back, shocked.

Amelia stood and let the sweater fall from her shoulders.

"I'm still yours," she said. "Even when the world watches. Even when they try to strip that from us."

She straddled his lap and wrapped her arms around his neck and kissed him.

His hands trembled when he held her.

"You're calm." He said.

"Because I know the ending," she whispered.

His forehead dropped to hers.

"What is it?"

She smiled.

"I win."

* * *

The house was too quiet. Not the comforting kind of quiet they'd built together. This was the silence of something held too tightly and about to break.

Lucas hadn't spoken in over an hour. After the call with his team, he'd shut down. He sat now in the leather chair near the fireplace, legs spread and elbows on his knees. Still shirtless and his slacks undone at the waist.

Amelia stood in the door way, watching him. He looked like a man at war with himself.

Not a Dom. Not a protector. Not the man who commanded her breath and body. Just Lucas.

She stepped forward and he didn't move.

"I've called everyone I know," he said. "Everyone who owes me. People who don't even exist on paper anymore."

Amelia knelt beside him. "You think you failed me."

He didn't answer, she reached for his hand.

"You didn't."

"It happened under my watch."

"And I said yes," she said. "I said yes to everything you gave me. Every inch of rope, every mark and every thrust."

She looked up into his eyes. "And I would say yes again."

His throat worked around the words. "You don't understand what this has done to me."

"Then tell me."

Lucas's hands flexed uselessly against his thighs. Knuckles pale and tendons tight like wires straining to snap. His chest rose and fell in shallow bursts but no words came at first. His silence felt heavier then shouting.

When he finally spoke, his voice was low and raw.

"I want to kill him."

Amelia didn't flinch. "I know."

But Lucas shook his head. His eyes were unfocused as if he was seeing something she couldn't.

"No, Amelia. I need it. Not justice. Not defence." His breath caught. His fingers curled until his palms bled against his half healed cuts. "I need to feel him die."

She exhaled softly, stepping closer.

"Then you're human."

That broke him. His head snapped up, eyes glassy and she saw it. The tears he hadn't let fall. The shame curdling beneath his skin. The rage, endless and hungry with nowhere left to go but inside.

She didn't try to soothe him with words. She just stood, quiet and steady. Then she offered her hand.

Lucas stared at it like it was a blade aimed at his chest. His breathing roughened, his body rigid with the refusal to break.

He took her hand slowly. She led him through the hallways of his own estate like he was the one lost.

The bedroom was dark but warm. She undressed him slowly. Not like a lover but like a ritual.

Each button undone with care. Each sleeve slid off like she was peeling grief from his skin. When he was bare, she pressed her hands flat to his chest.

"You're still here," she said.

He closed his eyes. "I don't want to be strong tonight."

"Then don't be." She said as she pulled him to the bed and climbed in, drawing him down over her body. .

Not to dominate, not to surrender, just to hold.

Lucas wrapped his arms around her waist and buried his face in her neck. His body shook. Not from desire but from *too much.*

"I don't deserve you," he whispered.

She kissed his temple. "I didn't survive all of that to find someone easy."

He pulled back just enough to look at her.

His eyes were glassy.

"Please," he whispered.

She slid her hand down between them and found him hard.

Not because of lust but because he needed *release*.

She stroked him slowly and gently. His breath caught.

"I'm going to fuck you," she said softly.

He nodded, "please."

She turned him over and straddled him. Guided him inside her. They both gasped as their bodies joined together.

But this time there were no orders, no roles and no games. Just two people moving together as one. He clung to her as she rose him slow. Her hips moving with reverence, her body surrounding his like a balm.

When he came, it was silent. A full body quake, his hands shaking, his eyes clenched shut.

And then he wept.

She didn't say a word, just held him until the shaking stopped.

Twenty-Six

Chapter 26

The call came just after midnight.

Lucas was in the study, half-dressed, scrolling through satellite feeds from his security team. Amelia was asleep in their bed, bare skin tangled in dark sheets. One hand resting where his body should've been.

The encrypted line buzzed once.

Lucas answered on the second ring.

"Go."

The voice on the other end wasn't one of his usual operatives. It was the federal liaison assigned to Ethan's case.

"Mr Cross. I assume you're still acting under Amelia Monroe's legal protection directive?"

Lucas's blood turned to ice.

"What happened?"

"Ethan Walker escaped custody today."

Silence for a moment.

"He was being transferred for a secondary psych evaluation ahead of sentencing. He faked a medical event. EMTs were called. During transport, two federal officers were incapacitated. One EMT was found unconscious. The other, female, is missing."

Lucas didn't breathe.

"We believe she may have been assisting him. We are pulling video now. Her background is clean but..."

Lucas hung up, he didn't need to hear the rest. He already knew what was coming.

He didn't run to the bedroom, he walked quiet and measured. Like if he moved too fast, the world would collapse before he got there.

Amelia sat up the second he opened the door.

Her eyes found his in the dark.

"What is it?"

Lucas didn't speak. He just crossed the room and sat on the edge of the bed.

"Ethan's gone," he said quietly.

Her breath caught just once and then, "How?"

Lucas told her every detail. No sugar coating. And when he was done she didn't tremble.

Didn't panic and didn't scream.

She just nodded. "He's coming here," she said.

Lucas turned to her. "Not if I take you somewhere safe."

"No."

"Amelia..."

"I'm not hiding. Not anymore."

Lucas stood now pacing the room.

"I have safe houses in six countries. I can put you somewhere he'll never touch you."

She rose from the bed, completely bare, hair falling over her shoulders.

"I'm not running," she said. "Not again. Not ever."

He looked at her, like really looked and saw it. Not defiance, not recklessness but readiness.

Amelia stepped closer.

"He won't stop, Lucas. Not until one of us ends this. I'd rather it be me."

"You want to be bait."

"I am the obsession. That's not bait. That's inevitability."

His jaw clenched. "If he touches you…"

"He won't."

"You can't know that."

She stepped close enough to touch his chest. "I'm not the girl her broke."

She reached up and gripped his face. "And you're not the man who has to save me anymore."

Lucas closed his eyes and when he opened them something shifted. Not weakness but acceptance.

Of the war they were walking into together.

* * *

Lucas hadn't slept. By dawn the estate was transformed. Not visibly. There were no guards at the doors, no trucks in the driveway. But the infrastructure had changed.

A full surveillance team was on-site. Embedded in the estate's encrypted network. Private security contractors were patched into heat signatures, movement grids and external drones.

The east wing had been re secured. The mirror removed.

Lucas stood in the study. Barefoot, shirt open and a holster strapped across him.

Amelia entered without knocking.

"I want to see the map." She said.

Lucas didn't argue.

He waved a hand toward the display. A 3D projection unfolded in the air. Heat blips around the estate, a moving cluster of tracked satellite data over the last 24 hours.

"We've locked the perimeter down. No one in or out. Facial recognition scans every thirty seconds."

Amelia studied the movement paths.

"He'll still come."

"Yes, he will."

"He's not going to wait anymore."

Lucas's gaze slid to her and the ice in his eyes was absolute.

"No. He knows it's over."

She exhaled, steadying herself.

"He's not coming for just me, Lucas." Her voice was low, sharp as glass. "He's coming for us."

Later that night, the fire was low again. The command screens still glowing in the dark.

Lucas sat alone in the study, watching the loops. The heat maps. Every blink of movement catalogued and timed.

Then a ping.

Not an alert but a heartbeat.

One of his black-hat trackers sent a single pulse through the network. Lucas sat up. A lived feed opened. It was grainy at first but then it focused.

Outside the estate.

At the edge of the tree line. A figure. Not moving, just standing there watching.

Lucas stood, he tapped the line. "Are you seeing this?" he asked.

A voice came back. "Yes, sir. No movement for ten minutes. We have a drone repositioning. He knows we are watching."

"Good."

"Orders?"

Lucas stared at the screen and smiled. "Let him watch. He'll come in soon."

"And when he does?"

Lucas turned as Amelia stepped into the room beside him and said, "we close the door behind him."

Twenty-Seven

Chapter 27

The glow of the screen was the only light in the room. Everything else, curtains, windows, clocks was covered. Silence hummed. Not empty but electric. Breathing and watching.

The video paused. The timestamp bled in red from the corner of the screen.

Three weeks after the trial began.

Amelia knelt. She was naked and her head bowed. Lucas stood behind her, hand around her throat like she was his prayer.

Ethan stared. He had watched this frame for thirty-seven minutes.

He knew the exact tilt of her chin. The way her lips parted, not from pain but from pleasure. He knew the reflection in her eyes.

The twitch under his skin hadn't stopped in hours. He hit play again. The sound was low. Just breath and movement.

Her moan slipped through the speaker, soft and broken.

Lucas whispered something he couldn't make out.

Amelia nodded, like obedience and worship.

Ethan's nails scraped the desk. *She never looked at me like that, he* thought to himself.

He rewound and watched again. Slower this time. He zoomed in on her eyes, they were dilated and glazed.

"You let him erase me," he whispered.

The walls creaked or maybe he imagined it. Hard to tell anymore. The files were already open.

A folder labelled: **Control.**

Images. Clips. Moments she'd forgotten and moments she never knew he'd captured.

He'd kept it all. Not out of spite. Out of faith. She was his church once. His ritual. And he'd filmed every prayer.

Now she belonged to someone else. He opened the latest file.

A draft email. Untraceable address and encrypted dump link.

Targeted to a gossip site with no ethics and endless reach.

He hovered over the send button.

"This isn't revenge," he murmured. "This is confession, and she should be grateful I'm the one telling her story."

The cursor blinked.

"She thinks submission means power," he said softer now. "She forgot who taught her what pain was."

He ran a finger along the edge of the desk until it bled.

A small line of red. He didn't flinch. Pain, after all, was just punctuation.

He stared at the frame again.

Amelia, looking up at Lucas with tears in her eyes. But not broken. Full. Soft. Loved.

Something foreign twisted inside him.

"She was never like that with me," he whispered to himself. "But she will be again. When I take everything back."

He clicked send and smiled like a man who thought God had finally answered.

He leaned back in the cracked leather chair, one hand resting over his groin as the video looped silently.

Her mouth was open again. Her eyes full of something he didn't recognise. It wasn't fear. That made his skin crawl. Because he had broken her. He had made her.

Whatever Lucas had now, he was playing with a house someone else had built. And he was about to burn it down.

A flicker of movement caught the corner of his eye, just his own reflection in the dark window.

He didn't look like a prisoner anymore. He looked like the God she used to worship.

"Mine," he murmured.

The words didn't echo, they thudded like a hammer.

He stood, restless and walked to the metal shelf bolted to the wall.

Pulling a small black case from underneath. Inside, he kept mementos.

Things he used on her. The old leather belt, creased and bloodstained near the buckle. A photograph she never knew he took, her face blurred in motion, tear- streaked and wide eyed. And the necklace.

The thin silver chain she wore the night he first 'disciplined' her.

He held it up now. Letting it dangle between his fingers. A memory came. She'd screamed that night. Not from pleasure, not even from pain, not really. But from realisation.

He had held her down, in the bathtub. Water halfway up her nose, her wrists bruising under his hands as she kicked and gasped and finally went limp. And when she came up for air, choking and crying, he'd whispered, "You made me do that."

And the way she'd looked at him then, like she'd seen her own grave.

His cock twitched. He inhaled, slow and deep, the memory painting him hard.

Amelia. On her knees. Begging, bleeding and perfect.

They didn't understand. Not Lucas, not the world. That wasn't trauma. That was truth.

She belonged to the man who unmade her.

Not the one who tried to glue the pieces back together.

He moved to the desk, and clicked to open another file. This one labelled **Priestess.**

A sound file. Her voice, one he'd secretly recorded when she cried in the dark after sex. Whispering broken apologies to herself.

He played it. Static, then…

"I don't know who I am anymore. I can't tell if it's me or him but I keep going back. I think… I think maybe I deserve it."

His eyes fluttered shut.

He fisted himself through his pants, because it wasn't about sex. It was about obliteration. Amelia wasn't a woman. She was the altar.

And he still had the knife.

Twenty-Eight

Chapter 28

The morning mist hadn't lifted yet. It curled low over the grass like breath held too long. Clinging to the hedges and climbing roses that lined the estate's south garden. The air smelled of wet earth and early spring.

Amelia walked alone. Wrapped in a black cashmere shawl, boots soft over the gravel path. She hadn't told him where she was going. She didn't need to, not anymore.

Surveillance covered the grounds. Cameras in the trees and motion sensors in the soil. Lucas would know where she was.

Her thoughts were quiet and focused. There was peace in the garden or had been before Ethan's escape. Before the leak. Before the sound of phantom footsteps near the perimeter wall.

Before she started feeling *watched again.*

She followed the path around the far side of the property. It curved toward a small grove of trees at the edge of the forest line. Nothing special, just a place the sun touched differently in the morning. She stopped at the largest tree. That's when she saw it.

Pinned delicately between two low branches, caught in the crook of the bark like someone had placed it there.

It was a photograph. Amelia's breath caught as she stepped closer. The edges were worn and the gloss had faded. A small water stain in the top right corner but she knew the image instantly.

It was of her at nineteen. Out with friends at the pier. A plastic cup of soda in her hand and the night sky full of neon lights from the rides behind them. She was smiling, like really smiling. Hair windblown and her cheeks flushed. A moment from before everything changed.

She remembered this night.

She hadn't known Ethan very long. He was new then, charming and magnetic. He'd taken the photo when she wasn't looking, told her later he loved the way she looked when she was happy.

She hadn't seen it since and yet here it was. She didn't move for a full minute. Just stared at the photo then carefully, she reached out and plucked it free.

She turned and walked back to the house. Lucas was in the kitchen, pouring coffee when she walked in. He wore only dark track pants and the edge of a healing bruise across his side, a mark she'd put there with her teeth two nights ago.

He looked up as she entered. Her expression told him everything. She walked to the island and set the photo down between them and stepped back.

Lucas picked it up slowly and froze.

A beat of silence stretched between them and then he set the photo back down.

"Where?" he asked.

"Birch grove. It was on a low branch," she said.

Lucas's gaze sharpened. "Anyone else see it?"

She shook her head.

His eyes narrowed, already running scenarios. "Did you touch anything?"

"Just the photo."

He swore under his breath, pacing once, sharp and contained.

"Lucas." Her voice cut through the room. He blinked and looked at her.

"This is intimate," she said. "Not just a message. A memory. He's not sending a threat."

She reached over and tapped the photo with one finger.

"He's sending nostalgia."

Lucas's jaw tightened. "I want every camera log from the last six hours pulled and analysed. Thermal signature, audio loops. We've got to check the outer fence for breaches."

He was already reaching for his phone. Amelia walked around the counter and placed her hand over his.

He stopped moving, his body gone still in that dangerous way she knew too well.

Amelia lifted her chin, meeting his gaze. "I'm not afraid," she said.

Lucas's gaze cut through her, cold and unyielding. "You should be."

Her breath left her slow and steady. "I was once."

The air between them felt like glass, fragile and waiting to crack. But her eyes didn't waver. They were clear now, focused, lit with something he hadn't seen in her before.

"That girl, in that photo?" she whispered. "She's gone. She doesn't live here anymore."

Lucas stared at her and something inside him shifted. He turned the photo over. On the back, in Ethan's handwriting were three words:

I remember everything.

Lucas said nothing, Amelia reached up and plucked the photo from his hand and tore it up into little pieces. "I remember to." she said and walked away.

* * *

The garage was quiet. Not silent though. There was always a soft hum here, the low mechanical pulse of security sensors and atmospheric control. Lucas's estate didn't believe in anything as simple as off-switches. Every door, every engine, every blind spot was always awake.

Amelia stepped into the cool air barefoot, a mug of tea cupped between her palms. It had been two days since the photo. Since the moment Ethan told her without speaking, that he remembered everything.

Lucas hadn't let her out of his sight for more then twenty minutes at a time. She didn't protest but she still needed a moment alone.

The garage lights flickered on in a soft, silent sweep. Her car sat in the corner. Lucas rarely let her drive it anymore but she had come to check the glove compartment. A list she thought she might've left there.

Then she saw it. On the windshield. Nestled perfectly beneath the wiper blade.

A rose.

Deep red and fresh. It wasn't wrapped in plastic just the stem and thorns still intact.

No note, no message though. Not this time. Just a memory. Her breath caught not in fear but in recognition. This was the colour Ethan always chose.

After every breakdown, every twisted, manic fight. He'd show up with a single red rose tucked behind his back like a peace offering.

"It's just a fight, baby. You know how much I love you." He would say.

Amelia stepped closer. The petals were damp with condensation. She stared at the rose but didn't touch it. She reached into her back pocket and pulled out her phone.

Lucas answered on the first ring.

"Where are you?"

"Garage."

There was a pause and a rustle of movement on the other end.

"Talk to me."

Her throat felt tight. "There's a rose on my windshield."

Silence for a moment then his voice low, edged with steel: "Are you safe?"

"Yes." She could picture his jaw clenching, the way his

shoulders squared when he was holding rage in check.

"I'm coming to you." The line went dead.

Amelia didn't move. She stood on the cold concrete, steam curling from her mug of tea and the rose bleeding its colour across the windshield. The hum of the garage lights filled the silence until the side door opened.

Lucas stepped inside. Shirtless with a gun in one hand, rage coiled tight in his body. His eyes swept the space once. Every shadow, every corner before they landed on her.

In two strides he was in front of her. His free hand gripped her arm, scanning her like he needed proof she was whole. Only when he found no blood, no break did his chest ease by an inch.

"You think this is helping?" His voice was a growl now, meant for the air more than for her.

Amelia reached up, slow, steady and placed her hand on his face. He froze under the touch, rage still crackling off him.

"It's not helping me," she said softly. "It's helping him into a corner."

Lucas blinked and smiled. Sharp, dark and proud. "You're learning to hunt."

Amelia smiled back. "No," she said. "I'm learning to finish."

Twenty-Nine

Chapter 29

The security alert came just after 2:00 am.

A ping on Lucas's private tablet. A subtle red pulse in the corner of the screen labelled:

Gate Proximity- Breach: Level 1

He was out of bed in seconds. No panic, just motion. Like a predator responding to motion in the dark.

Amelia stirred, her hand reaching across the sheets to where his body had been. "Lucas?"

"Stay here," he said quietly. "I'll call you if it's anything."

She didn't argue but she sat up alert and ready.

Lucas grabbed his weapon from the nightstand, thumbed the safety off and padded barefoot through the hallway. He didn't turn on lights, his eyes didn't need them.

By the time he reached the main control room, the monitor was already cycling through feeds. One froze.

Front gate, just past the tree line. Nothing moving and

nothing too obvious. But something was different.

He rewound the footage.

1:57 am, empty.

1:58, still empty.

1:59, movement.

Just a flicker of a shadow. A figure near the edge of the fence. Half crouched. Then they were gone again.

By the time the on-site guard reached the spot, the figure was gone. But something had been left behind.

Lucas watched as the guard retrieved it and delivered it inside a sealed evidence sleeve. His face was pale beneath his tactical cap.

By 2:11, it was in Lucas's hands.

A single sheet of white paper with four words, written across the centre in Ethan's handwriting.

I'm still listening.

He walked into the bedroom with the paper in hand. Amelia sat on the edge of the bed, already dressed in one of his black shirts. Her hair was down and her spine was straight.

He handed it to her without speaking.

She read it once but she didn't react. No sound, no shifting in her breathing.

"How close was he?" she asked.

"Fifteen feet from the main gate."

"No camera caught his face?"

"Only shadow."

"Then he's better then I remember."

Lucas crouched in front of her, his jaw tight and every line of his body wound like a spring. The silence stretched. Amelia could feel the heat of him, the rage simmering just beneath the surface, begging to be unleashed.

"You still think we let him play this out?" His voice low and dangerous.

Amelia met his gaze and really looked at him. Past the anger, past the control he fought to hold. She saw the man who would burn the world to protect her and still.

"Yes."

Lucas stood, pacing. "He's escalating. Leaving notes, listening devices. You want him closer? You want to invite him in?"

She followed him with her eyes and said softly: "Yes, because every time he leaves something behind, he forgets he's leaving a trail. I want him to think I'm soft."

Lucas stepped in. His voice low. "You're not."

"No. But if he thinks I am?" She looked up, her eyes burning. "He'll stop running."

They stood face to face. Both dangerous and both calm.

Then Lucas whispered: "You're not prey anymore."

Amelia smiled. "I know."

* * *

The control room lights buzzed low, blue screens casting a sterile glow across the stone walls. The surveillance feeds flickered. The main gate looped on repeat.

Lucas stood in front of the display, jaw clenched so tightly the muscle ticked beneath his skin. Behind him, Amelia leaned against the door frame.

The torn pieces of Ethan's note lay in a sealed evidence bag beside Lucas's hand.

He hadn't spoken in ten minutes, then: "He's in range."

Amelia didn't move. "Not close enough."

Lucas turned. His face was quiet. "If I go now, I can intercept him. I have the trajectory mapped. I've got three ground teams who can sweep the ridge. By sunrise, he's either caught or dead."

"You're assuming he wants to run."

"He's taunting us."

"No," she said softly. "It's worse, he's lingering."

Lucas crossed to the centre of the room.

"You want me to wait. While he plays with our lives. Our fucking bedroom. While he listens to you breathe and watches you walk through this house."

"Yes."

His voice dropped. "You think patience will save us?"

"I think your rage will kill you."

That stopped him. She stepped into the room now. "I know that look in your eyes," she said. "It's the same one I saw in the mirror before I finally left him. That look of quiet murder."

Lucas didn't speak. Amelia walked up to him, chest to chest.

"You're unravelling," she said. "But not because you're scared. Because you can't touch him yet."

He reached up and fisted a hand in her hair, not rough, just there.

"I want to tear the skin from his face," he whispered. "I want to hear him beg."

Her breath hitched but not from fear, from recognition. "I know," she said. "But I want something worse."

Lucas's eyes narrowed. "Worse?"

"I want him to think he's still in control. I want him to get comfortable. I want him to watch me undress from the trees and convince himself I'm still his."

She stepped even closer. Her voice like a blade. "And then I want to see my eyes when he dies. I want that to be the last thing he ever sees."

Lucas inhaled slowly, his hand still tangled in her hair. "You'd kill him?"

"Yes." Her voice didn't waver.

Lucas's eyes searched her face for hesitation, for the tremor that used to haunt her but he found none. "You'd look him in the eyes and pull the trigger?"

Amelia smiled. It wasn't soft, wasn't sweet. It was sharp, feral, the kind of smile born from scars rather then innocence. "I wouldn't flinch."

Lucas stared at her for a moment, then he laughed low and dark.

"Jesus Christ, I love you," he said.

She took his face in her hands. "Then let me lead." She kissed his mouth, not soft, not sweet. Like war and devotion. Then she whispered against his lips, "let him feel close. That's when he gets sloppy."

Lucas dropped his forehead to hers and closed his eyes. "And when he does?"

She smiled but not soft.

"We finish it."

Chapter 30

The kitchen was sunlit, quiet and filled with the soft clinking of glass and the low hum of the kettle warming on the stove.

Amelia stood barefoot in one of Lucas's sweaters, sleeves hanging past her wrists while she sliced strawberries.

The security chime sounded and Lucas appeared from the hallway, hair still damp from the shower. "She's here," he said simply.

Amelia's eyes lit up, she dropped the knife and ran.

Sophia stood in the main foyer, black boots, dark jeans and a fitted blazer. She looked like someone who could argue a murder case and then burn the courthouse down afterward.

Amelia didn't hesitate. She collided into her best friend. Sophia wrapped her arms around her without a word and held her so tight it hurt.

"Jesus, Monroe. You're even hotter when you're not bleeding in a courtroom."

Amelia laughed. "Still dramatic."

"Always." Sophia cupped her face. "And still yours."

Lucas approached, silent as ever.

Sophia turned to him, eyes sharp but warmer now.

"Lucas." His name was less a greeting and more a test.

"Sophia." His reply was flat and measured. Like two wolves circling.

Her eyes flicked over him, sharp and unapologetic. Then her lips curved.

"You still fucking my girl right?"

Lucas blinked once, no hesitation, no shame. "Everyday."

Sophia's smirk sharpened, approval sparking like flint in her gaze. "Good."

Amelia stood between them, a silent pulse of amusement thrumming in her chest.

Sophia tossed her blazer over the back of a chair. Amelia trailed her into the kitchen, still grinning.

Lucas stayed a step behind, silent and watchful. But the women, they slipped straight back into an orbit that belonged to them alone.

Sophia plopped down at the table, fingers drumming on the wood.

"You still cut the crusts off?"

Amelia laughed, louder then she had in weeks. "Only if they're burnt."

"God, remember when you set the toaster on fire?" Sophia leaned back, head thrown back in laughter. "Whole dorm smelled like smoke for two days."

Amelia pressed a hand over her face, giggling. "That wasn't me, that was you! You forgot the Pop Tarts."

"Semantics." Sophia waved a hand, grinning. "I had finals, Monroe. I was stressed."

Their laughter ricocheted through the kitchen. They moved easily from one memory to the next. Sneaking vodka into water bottles at concerts, to crying on the bathroom floors over boys who hadn't mattered.

Every memory was a lifeline, tugging Amelia back toward the girl she had been before Ethan.

Lucas leaned against the counter, arms crossed and silent. But there was something in his eyes as he watched her laugh with her best friend, something almost reverent.

For a little while, Amelia forgot about shadows at the gate and notes left on windshields. She just remembered who she was and who had always loved her.

When Sophia rose to leave, dusk was falling.

"I'll grab a hotel nearby," she said.

Lucas offered her a room but she refused.

"You need space for the war coming," she said. "I'm just your favourite general. I'll be nearby."

They hugged again, this one tighter. Amelia's fingers didn't want to let go. Sophia pulled back and touched her face.

"Call me when you forget who you are."

Amelia nodded. "I won't forget again."

* * *

Later that night- The Call.

The call came at 11:32pm.

Lucas answered it in two rings.

Amelia sat up in bed before he even spoke.

"Talk to me," Lucas said into the phone.

Sophia's voice crackled through the line. "I'm okay but you need to hear this."

"What happened?"

"I stopped for gas, got back to my car and the window was smashed. Purse untouched, nothing was stolen."

Lucas was already moving and Amelia was behind him, her heart pounding.

"But there was something left on the driver's seat."

Lucas's voice dropped to a growl. "What?"

"A note, folded in quarters."

Amelia's mouth went dry.

"It said: "Wrong girl. Right leverage.""

Then there was silence. Sophia's voice came back smaller this time.

"He wanted me to call her."

Amelia sat down hard on the edge of the bed. Her hands shaking but it wasn't from fear, it was from rage.

Lucas knelt in front of her, his voice low and steady.

"We'll find him and I'll end this."

Amelia didn't look at him, she stared straight ahead. "No I will. He's not yours to kill, Lucas. He's mine."

Thirty-One

Chapter 31

Amelia sat on the kitchen counter, barefoot and wrapped in Lucas's hoodie, watching Sophia pour a third glass of wine.

"You're spiralling," Sophia said. "You only wear his hoodie when you're trying not to come undone."

Amelia half-smiled. "I thought that was your job."

Sophia passed her the glass, then leaned on the counter beside her. "Tonight, I'm off-duty. Just your emotionally unstable best friend with questionable taste in wine."

"Did I ever tell you about Jamie?" Sophia said casually.

Amelia blinked. "Your ex?"

Sophia's mouth twisted. "One of them. The one who said if I ever told anyone what he did to me, he'd sue me for defamation. Said I was 'too dramatic to be taken seriously.' "

A pause.

"I left a job I loved for him. Burned bridges, moved cities and when it was over, I didn't even scream. Just disappeared because I thought no one would believe me."

Amelia's throat tightened. "Why didn't you ever say anything?"

"I didn't want you to see me broken." Sophia's eyes flickered to hers, glassy. "But you're showing me there's power in being honest. Even when it hurts."

Amelia reached out and laced her fingers with Sophia's. "You're not broken, you're brave."

Sophia set down her glass. "Good, because I'm about to declare war."

She pulled out her phone. "I've been drafting a post. I'm tagging Ethan, his team and every outlet that ran that leaked footage."

"You sure?" Amelia whispered.

Sophia's voice was steel. "He doesn't get to weaponize your pain. Not on my watch."

She hit post.

The wine bottle was empty, but neither of them felt drunk anymore. Just tired. Heavy with truths that had finally been spoken.

At some point, the laughter faded and the talking slowed. Their heads tipped together on the couch, fingers still laced between them. Sleep stole them without warning.

Lucas found them like that hours later. Amelia curled into Sophia's side, both of them wrapped in the ghost of too much wine and too many memories.

He didn't wake Sophia, just draped a blanket over her to keep her warm. Then he bent and gathered Amelia against his chest, the faintest murmur leaving her lips as she nuzzled closer. By the time he laid her beneath the sheets, she was already lost to dreams.

Amelia stirred beneath the thick cotton sheets. Lucas's hoodie was tangled around her waist. Padding into the kitchen she found Sophia putting the kettle on.

"You're up early," Amelia murmured.

Sophia glanced over. "Couldn't sleep. Brain's too loud."

She handed Amelia a mug of chamomile tea.

"Thanks," Amelia said curling into the corner of the couch. "You okay?"

Sophia hesitated. "Yeah, just thinking."

They sat in silence for a minute, the quiet not heavy just real. Finally Sophia spoke. "You ever imagine what happens after this? Like really after?"

Amelia blinked. "Sometimes."

Sophia turned toward her. "Okay, no trauma talk. No legal war. Just fantasy. What's the first thing you want when it's all over?"

Amelia leaned back, closing her eyes. "A real night of sleep. One where I'm not bracing for ghosts."

Sophia smiled. "And after that?"

"A bath in a five star hotel. Big enough to drown in, with lavender oil and no one watching."

"That's very specific."

"I've had time to think." Amelia laughed softly.

"You know what I want?" Sophia chuckled, pulling her knees to her chest.

Amelia looked over. "What?"

"To disappear for a month. No social media. No headlines. Just me, a suitcase and a fake name."

"Are you secretly a spy?" Amelia joked.

Sophia smirked. "No, just a woman who's tried of being brave for everyone else."

Amelia's chest ached. "You've always been brave for me."

Sophia's voice softened. "I'd do it again, every time."

Amelia reached out, their fingers tangling over the edge of the couch. "I want us to go somewhere together. A girls' trip. Beach, books and wine that costs too much."

"I want a beach bonfire," Sophia said, her eyes lighting. "Music, and dancing barefoot. No one touching us unless we invite it."

"And I want to get drunk enough to sing karaoke." Amelia added with a smile.

Sophia raised an eyebrow." You sing?"

"If you dance."

"Deal."

They laughed a real belly-deep laugh. Then Sophia's smile faded just a little. "Promise me we'll do it."

"We will," Amelia said, without hesitation.

Sophia looked away. "I don't know why, but I feel like time's moving too fast. Like we're running out of it."

Amelia's throat tightened. "Don't say that."

"I mean it in a good way," Sophia lied. "Like maybe it means something's about to break open."

Amelia leaned into her side, cheek against her shoulder. "We'll have that trip. The ocean, the songs, the sunburns. All of it."

Sophia swallowed hard. "Okay."

They sat like that for a while. Watching the sunrise over the edge of the world. Two women who had survived too much, daring to dream in the pause between storms.

Thirty-Two

Chapter 32

They sat across from each other in the study. The lights were dim. The air between them heavy with unsaid things. Amelia was barefoot and still in the same clothes from last night. Lucas sat like he always did, commanding and unreadable.

Except now she was the one giving orders.

"You sure?" he asked.

Amelia nodded. "Yes."

"You want him close."

"I want him trapped."

Lucas studied her, this version of her wasn't trembling, wasn't reacting.

She was calculating and it hit him all at once.

She wasn't healing anymore. She was preparing. Amelia leaned forward and laid out her plan:

"We let the next message come through. Whatever it is. We let him place it and we make him feel safe and confident.

Watched but not stopped."

Lucas arched a brow. "And then?"

"I answer him." Amelia said, cold and direct. "I write him back."

Lucas blinked. "You want to correspond with him?"

"I want to bait him. Intimately and personally."

Lucas's jaw tightened. He wasn't sure if he liked this.

"You're afraid he'll get in my head again." She said, noticing his tension.

Lucas didn't deny it.

"I know what he is," Amelia said. "I'm not afraid of his words. I've already lived inside them and I survived."

He leaned back, arms crossed. "You're asking me to let him get close enough to touch you again."

"No," she said. "I'm asking you to help me touch him."

Lucas looked at her and something in him shifted. He nodded once and then rose from his chair. Walking around the table, stopped in front of her and knelt. "I will be with you 100 percent."

"This ends with him dead," she whispered. "I want my hands on the knife."

Lucas looked up, eyes steady.

"Then I'll sharpen the blade for you."

Amelia sat at Lucas's desk, pen in hand. Ethan's notes had always been clean and precise. Violence dressed as romance.

Lucas stood behind her.

She whispered, "What should I write?"

He leaned in close. "Say what he's waiting to hear."

She nodded and then put pen to paper writing:

I miss the way you watched me. Are you watching now?

She paused and looked at Lucas.

"More," he said.

Amelia added:

You always said I was beautiful when I cried. You'd be proud. I've been crying a lot lately.

Lucas's hand brushed her shoulder, steadying her. "That's enough for the first strike," he murmured. "It's bait, not surrender."

Amelia folded the paper and Lucas sealed it himself. When he looked at her, something dark flickered behind his eyes.

"What?" she asked.

"I should've killed him when I had the chance," he said.

Amelia didn't argue instead she just reached for his hand.

"Then help me kill him now, my way."

The message was dropped near the same gate Ethan had used last. Lucas's team pulled back but the cameras were still watching.

The note was gone by morning. No prints, no tracks but something else was left behind.

A single black ribbon, tied around a small silver locket.

Amelia opened it. Inside was a photo of her and Sophia. It was a reminder of what could be taken.

Lucas saw her hands shake.

"Do you want to stop?" he asked.

Amelia looked up at him, eyes dark and angry.

"No, now I know where to aim."

***

It arrived just as the sky turned the colour of old bruises, dusk sliding over the estate like a quiet threat.

Amelia was alone when the knock came. Three precise taps. One of Lucas's men stood at the door. Gloved and silent. He handed her a sealed envelope, his expression unreadable. She took it without a word and slowly opened it.

You've always looked your best in a trap.

Her breath hitched. He wasn't angry, he was *aroused*.

I remember the way you held your breath when you lied to me.
You'd forget, sometimes that I could hear it.
I always knew when you were pretending.

Her fingers curled around the edge of the letter.

Does Lucas know what you sound like when you come and want to die at the same time?

Her stomach twisted. Lucas had never hurt her like that. But Ethan?

He made pain an art form. Taught her to moan and flinch at once.

Tell him you're not clean. Tell him I already stripped you bare, that I know the real you. The you that craved the cruelty. The you that begged when there was no safe word.

Tears didn't fall, she was past tears now.

You think he owns you now? You think submission makes you safe? But you were never safe. You were mine when you were at your most ashamed. Come home, little dove. You're just playing dress up.

She didn't remember standing but she heard the letter burn. The sound of paper catching on fire and curling black.

The edges glowing like the heat behind her eyes.

Lucas walked in just in time to see the ashes fall in the fireplace. He didn't speak, she turned to him and for a moment she looked haunted.

"He's not trying to find me," she said.

Lucas nodded. "He's trying to pull you back."

Amelia wrapped her arms around herself. "He knows how to sound like safety."

Lucas stepped close and reached for her face. She leaned into the touch and that broke something in him. "I hate that he knows you so well."

"He doesn't know me now though, he knew the old, weak me."

She straightened and lifted her chin to meet his gaze. "I'm not that small weak girl anymore."

Lucas exhaled like he'd been drowning, then he knelt at her feet and laid his forehead to her stomach. Not out of dominance but out of surrender.

"I'd kill him a thousand times, if it meant keeping you this strong."

Amelia ran her fingers through his hair.

"I don't want you to kill him." She looked down at him and her voice turned cold like ice. "I want you to watch him beg before I do it myself."

Thirty-Three

Chapter 33

The clock on the mantel ticked, soft and rhythmic. Lucas was upstairs on a call with his security team.

Amelia stood in the library, one hand resting on the desk, the other thumbing the edge of a photo she and Sophia had taken years ago.

Sophia had sent it to her last week.

Don't forget who you were before he broke you, was written on the back. Amelia smiled faintly. Then her phone buzzed. Sophia was calling.

"Tell me you're not still working." Amelia teased.

Sophia's laugh was quiet and hollow.

"I was going to lie and say I'd just had a glass of wine but you'd hear it."

Amelia sat down slowly.

"Everything okay?"

A pause. Sophia didn't answer right away.

"I think someone's been in my hotel room."

The air shifted. Amelia's spine straightened.

"Did you call security?"

"I can't prove it. Nothing's missing but the folder I left on the desk was turned. The tag on my bag was clipped off. My…my toothbrush was wet."

Silence.

"Lucas can…"

"No," Sophia's voice calm and firm. "Not yet. I don't want to start a panic. I'm going to head to the courthouse early. I'll stay in public."

Amelia's throat tightened.

"Soph…"

"I'm okay. I'm just being careful."

Another pause. Then softer: "I love you. You know that right?"

Amelia blinked. "You're coming back."

Sophia laughed again, too soft. "Of course I am."

The line clicked. Dead. No static, no goodbye.

Amelia stood in the hallway, phone still pressed to her ear, her other hand braced on the wall like the house was moving underneath her.

"She's gone."

Lucas stepped closer. "What happened?"

"She said someone had been in her room. She was scared but she wouldn't say it out loud."

"Where was she?"

"Courthouse. That's where she was going."

Lucas pulled his phone out and hit a code. Security lockdown protocols went live in the background.

"She'll be found."

They found Sophia's car forty-two minutes later.

Lucas's private team traced her last GPS ping to a public parking structure just off the courthouse plaza. Four levels of exposed concrete, dim yellow lighting and too much space between the shadows.

Level 3, space 27B.

The car was parked straight. The engine cool. Lucas stood beside the vehicle, his team flanking him like wolves waiting for the order to kill.

Amelia stayed by the elevator, heart hammering like it was trying to claw out of her chest.

She already knew, she didn't know how but she knew.

Lucas opened the driver's side door. Inside Sophia's purse was neatly tucked in the passenger seat. Her laptop bag was closed and a coffee cup in the holder was still warm.

Her phone was gone. But she hadn't run, she hadn't fought. If she had, it wouldn't be this quiet. Then Lucas saw the envelope.

He opened it and Amelia watched his jaw tighten. He read the message aloud.

"Now you remember how it feels to lose someone who doesn't come back."

Amelia didn't cry, not yet. She walked over slowly, heels echoing off the concrete but her chest was already tight, breath coming too fast. Her hands brushed Lucas's as she took the note, gripping it like it might still be warm from Ethan's fingers.

Her voice cracked before she could stop it. "We have to get

her back, Lucas. Now. Before he...."

She cut herself off, jaw locking.

They searched the building, every stairwell, every floor and found nothing. No blood, no struggle just absence. That was worse.

Amelia stood outside the structure, arms crossed over her chest, wind blowing her hair across her face. She didn't speak, until one of the guards approached. They had something.

Drone footage, near the estate by the forest edge.

They drove back to the estate in silence. Lucas kept one had on the wheel, the other on her thigh, grounding and steadying her. But Amelia didn't lean in this time. She was too still and too quiet.

Because the moment the guard stepped forward, holding the tablet like it weighed more then tech should, she already knew.

Something had happened to Sophia. And whatever was on that footage? It wasn't going to be survivable.

They found her in the woods. Not far from the estate. Lucas's perimeter team picked up a heat signature that had gone cold. A body left where a drone wouldn't spot it, but close enough that they eventually would find it.

Ethan had wanted her found. He had timed it.

Her boots sank slightly into the moss. Each breath felt borrowed. The woods were too quiet, like the trees themselves were watching.

And then she saw it. The swing. And the body wasn't moving.

Her throat was slashed. Eyes swollen shut and her mouth

was sewn closed with thick black thread. Not neat, not surgical just cruel.

The threads cut into the skin like barbed wire, dried blood caked at the corners of her lips. Her hands had been broken. Her fingers bent at unnatural angles and the nails torn off.

Her blazer was torn and the shirt soaked with blood. But her face had been cleaned. And over her head, stapled to the tree behind her, was a single sheet of paper. Lucas reached for it, his hands trembling.

He read it aloud.

"She was too loud."

Amelia didn't move. She just stood there, staring at her best friend. At the woman who had held her through panic attacks and broken nights.

The woman who never left. Until now.

Lucas stepped toward her and reached for her arm. Amelia's legs gave out. She fell to her knees in the mud with a sound like something torn from the gut.

A scream that wasn't just a scream.

It was a sob so deep it didn't rise, it collapsed.

Sophia had just punched a boy for grabbing Amelia's arm too hard at the school dance. She'd smiled and said, "Nobody touches my girl without permission."

And now that same girl sat tied to a swing with silence stitched into her face.

"No," Amelia whispered. "No….no…no…no."

Mud soaked into her jeans, but she didn't care. Her fingers clawed at the earth like she could bury the image if she dug deep enough.

Lucas caught her before she tipped forward completely, but she fought him. Beat her fists against his chest.

"She was mine! She was mine! He doesn't get to… he doesn't get to take her too!"

"She promised me we'd make it out. That there would be sunrises and beach wine and bad karaoke."Her voice cracked.

"Now there's just dirt and stitches where her voice used to be!"

Lucas didn't speak. He just held her tighter until the fight ran out. Until she sobbed into his shirt with the kind of sound that breaks goddamn planets.

Amelia didn't speak for hours. Lucas brought her inside, wrapped her in a blanket and sat her by the fire.

She didn't move, didn't even blink. Just stared into the flames like they might erase what she'd seen.

The guards cleared the perimeter. The team swept the woods. Sophia's body was taken to a secure location, pending an autopsy.

Lucas stayed close enough to protect.

She finally spoke just past midnight.

"I wrote him first." Her voice low and hoarse.

Lucas looked up from across the room. She didn't meet his eyes.

"I wanted him to come closer. I wanted to make him sloppy. I thought….I thought if I baited him, I'd get the upper hand."

Her fingers dug into the blanket. "She didn't want me to go after him like this. She told me to stay human."

Lucas walked over to her, kneeling in front of her.

Amelia shook her head. "You don't understand, he killed her

because of me. Because I said I wanted to end him. Because I stopped hiding." Her voice broke. "I dragged her into this."

"She chose to stand beside you."

"She didn't choose to die in a fucking swing with her mouth sewn shut!"

The words tore out of her, wild and ugly.

Lucas didn't flinch, he took her anger because she needed to throw the pain somewhere.

She stood suddenly, throwing the blanket off, pacing in front of the fire like something in her was breaking apart in real time.

"I let him get inside my head again. I let him make me believe I was the one in control."

Lucas stood slowly. "You are in control."

She turned to him.

"Then why is she dead?"

Silence. Amelia's chest heaved. Tears burned down her cheeks.

"I thought I could beat him at his own game," she whispered. "But he doesn't play games."

She looked at Lucas now, full and unflinching. "He burns everything."

Lucas stepped forward, took her hands and held them tight even when she tried to pull away.

"You're right," he said.

That startled her.

"You're right, Amelia. You provoked him, you challenged him and you woke the monster up."

Her eyes filled with tears again.

"And now," he continued, voice low, steady and fierce. "Now you finish him."

He let go of her hands and reached for the small drawer beneath the fireplace ledge. Pulling out a gun and pressed it into her hands.

She stared down at it, feeling the weight in her hands.

"You don't run now," he said. "You don't cry."

He cupped her face and kissed her forehead like something holy.

"You kill him."

Thirty-Four

Chapter 34

The war table was lit from below, sleek black glass embedded with real-time feeds, security overlays, thermal data and motion grids.

It had always been Lucas's space, but tonight Amelia was at the head.

She was wearing black leggings, a simple cotton top and her hair twisted into a knot at the base of her skull. No jewellery, no makeup.

She didn't need armour, she was the weapon now.

Lucas leaned against the far wall, arms crossed and jaw tight. He hadn't said a word since the team assembled.

Amelia scanned the room. Five of Lucas's operatives stood ready and silent. Waiting for commands they were used to taking from someone else. But not tonight.

Tonight the orders came from her.

She could still feel Sophia's warmth in the sweater she hadn't taken off. Could still hear the swing creaking in the dark.

Her voice had been sewn shut but Amelia's wasn't.

She tapped the screen and the feed changed.

The garden, the perimeter path and the swing.

"This is where it started," she said. "The photo, the rose and the note. She looked up.

"Ethan used it as an opening. We're going to close it."

Lucas tilted his head slightly. "How?"

"We open it wider."

She turned, activated the interactive map and zoomed in on a small clearing just beyond the western edge of the greenhouse.

"Here. We leave the gate ajar. Half a meter. Just enough to say we forgot. We reduce the patrol cycle, give him a blind spot."

One of the guards, Mason, frowned. "He'll know it's a trap."

Amelia's voice didn't waver. "He'll think mine. Not yours. Not Lucas's but mine."

She looked back at Lucas now.

"Because he still believes I'm too emotional to build this. That I'm still afraid."

Lucas met her gaze. There was something quiet there. Fierce and something else. Grief.

Because the woman standing in front of him now was nothing like the one he held in trembling arms just days ago.

Amelia tapped the map again.

"We flood the greenhouse with heat and proximity triggers. No security team inside. Just me. Unarmed."

Mason stepped forward. "Absolutely not."

Lucas didn't speak.

Amelia looked up.

"I won't wear a wire. I won't carry a gun. He'll scan me and he will know."

Another silence and then Lucas spoke. "Then what happens?"

Amelia turned slowly.

"I talk to him."

"And if he tries to kill you?"

She didn't blink. "Then I let him get close enough to try."

Lucas dismissed the team ten minutes later.

He didn't look at anyone but her as the door closed behind them.

They were alone now and for a moment, the room was quiet again.

"You're not scared," he said.

"No."

"Not even a little?"

She stepped around the table and closed the distance between them. "I was scared when I watched him rip pieces of me apart and leave them on the floor like confetti. I was scared when I forgot how to sleep without a light on."

She looked at him and her voice steady now. "But now I know what I look like covered in someone else's blood."

"When I saw what he did to her. When I imagined cutting the breath out of him with my own hands…."

Lucas's breath stuttered. He brushed her jaw with his thumb. "I almost don't recognise you."

"You're not supposed to." She rested her forehead

to his and her voice dropped.

"You fell in love with the woman I was learning to become. But now what you're looking at the woman he created. And I won't apologise for it."

* * *

He watched the feed in silence. The greenhouse glowed like a heartbeat in the dark. The gate had been left ajar. Deliberately. A rookie mistake, if she was still the girl he remembered. But this wasn't a mistake.

It was an invitation and Ethan loved invitations.

He leaned back in the cracked leather chair, fingers drumming against his thigh. She was pretending to be strong, pretending she could out manoeuvre him. Trying to be the hunter.

But she'd forgotten something important. He made her. He taught her how to kneel, how to cry and how to bleed pretty and beg prettier.

And now she wanted to bait him?

He smiled.

Let her. Because he wasn't coming for her body this time. He was coming for her soul.

Thirty-Five

Chapter 35

The garden was wet with morning fog. The grass cold beneath Amelia's bare feet, soaking the hem of her pants as she walked alone across the manicured lawn.

She carried no weapons, no protection, just a small bundle of wildflowers clutched in her hand. She found the stone near the centre of the clearing. Lucas had placed it there quietly. A single square of white marble, polished smooth.

No last name, no inscription, just one word carved deep:
SOPHIA

Amelia knelt and set the flowers down. Resting her palm over the cool, damp stone.

She didn't cry, not here. There was something sacred about this silence, something she didn't want to ruin with crying.

"I should've stopped," she whispered. Her voice barely carried.

"I should've known he'd come for you. I should've never written him that fucking letter."

She closed her eyes.

"I kept telling myself I was strong enough. That I was becoming something that could stop him and you just wanted me to survive."

Amelia paused, and brushed a leaf of the headstone.

"I think you knew this might happen. I think that's why you came anyway. Because you couldn't let me fight without someone remembering who I used to be."

The fog clung to her skin. "I'm not that girl anymore."

She reached into her pocket and pulled out a silver chain. Sophia's necklace.

It had been in the envelope Ethan left on her body. Wrapped around the message like a noose.

Amelia placed it gently across the top of the marble.

"But I'll make sure he knows your name when he dies."

She leaned forward and pressed her forehead to the stone and whispered:

"Speak through me when I kill him."

From the edge of the garden, Lucas watched. He didn't move, didn't call out. He just watched the woman he loved mourn her best friend with silence and vengeance braided together.

And for the first time since this began, he was afraid of her. Not because she was dangerous, but because now she was unstoppable.

* * *

Amelia sat at the table with a single piece of paper in front of her. The scratch of pen on paper was the only sound. It didn't feel like writing, it felt like bleeding. Each word carved into the page like a knife into bone.

You killed the last person who knew the version of me you wanted to keep. She was the last echo of who I was before you. You tried to erase me, piece by piece. But you forgot what happens when you destroy someone with nothing left to lose.

She paused, then added:

You're not coming for Amelia Monroe anymore. She's already dead. What's left of her is what you made. And it remembers everything.

She folded it in half and wrapped it in a black silk tie.

Lucas entered the room and she handed him the message.

"Deliver it," she said. "same place her left her. The swing."

He looked into her eyes, "You're ready, aren't you?"

Amelia nodded. "There will be no more warnings, the next time I see him. I put him in the ground."

Thirty-Six

Chapter 36

The estate was silent. Outside, the moon was buried behind clouds, casting long shadows through the glass walls of the bedroom. Everything was soft and grey.

Amelia stood near the windows, her arms crossed and her muscles aching from the hours of training.

Behind her, Lucas waited.

He hadn't touched her since the plan was set. Not because he didn't want her. God, he did. But the fire in her gaze unsettled something in him, because the woman in front of him wasn't his to soothe anymore. She was something forged.

Now she turned to him, barefoot and hair loose over her shoulders.

Wearing only one of his black shirts and a look he hadn't seen before.

"I need you tonight," she said softly. "Before I forget what mercy tastes like."

Lucas moved toward her like a man obeying gravity.

"You want comfort?"

She shook her head slowly. "I want to be yours. One more time before I walk into the storm I might not survive."

His breath caught. He didn't want to think about this being the last time he might get to hold her.

Lucas stepped close, his fingers brushed the hem of her shirt, lifting it slowly. She let him, no tension, no fear, just breath.

The fabric dropped behind her like silence. Her skin marked from sparring, faded along her ribs.

Lucas's chest rose with the force of his restraint. He slid her panties down her thighs and threw them to the side of the room. She stood naked in front of him. Lucas circled her slowly. His fingers brushed her spine, the nape of her neck and the inside of her elbow.

He touched her like a prayer.

"On the bed," he said low and steady. "Hands and knees."

She moved without hesitation. He let her feel the space between command and contact. Let her ache for what came next.

He undressed behind her. The sound of latex gloves snapping over his hands echoed through the room. Then the first strike.

His palm against her ass, loud and sharp. She moaned. He slapped her again and again. Each slap a punctuation mark. A reminder. *You're here, you're real and you're still yours.*

"You want to forget the pain of the world?" He growled behind her. "I'll give you pain with a purpose."

He didn't spank her to punish, he spanked her to anchor her. Then the lubricant came, cold. Then two fingers inside her, no warning, no buildup just full.

"Count."

Her breath hitched. "One, Sir."

He pushed deeper and her thighs began to tremble. "Two…."

Her body jolted, a strangled sound escaping, "Three…."

Lucas's mouth was at her ear now, his voice a growl that vibrated through her bones.

"You'll feel full before I even fuck you."

"Yes, Sir…yes…please…"

He pulled out suddenly and her body ached at the loss. He yanked her by her hair bringing her up right. Shoving his fingers into her mouth. "Taste yourself."

She did, sucking her juices off his fingers, her eyes locking onto to his.

"You're not soft anymore," he whispered. "But God, I missed this version of you."

Then he threw her down, flat on her back and tied her hands above her head. Bending her knees up to her chest.

"I'm going to fuck you until you forget who you are."

"Please…" she begged.

He lined himself up, pressing the tip of his cock against her entrance.

"Tell me what you are."

"I'm yours." Her voice was raw and almost breaking.

"Louder," he demanded.

Her eyes squeezed shut and he whole body shook.

"I'm yours, Sir."

A pause, just long enough for her to feel the weight of her own words.

And then he buried himself in her. Amelia screamed not

from pain but from release.

His hands clamped to her hips, dragging her back onto him as though he couldn't get close enough.

He fucked her hard, every thrust claiming her more.

"This isn't mercy," he snarled. "This is worship. This is *church.*"

She was soaked, dripping with need. His name caught on her tongue like a vow.

She came once, shaking and then again sobbing.

He didn't stop until he spilled inside her, growling her name into her shoulder like it was the only word he knew.

He untied her gently and lifted her like she weighed nothing.

He drew her a bath and let her sit in his lap in the rising water.

She hadn't spoken since the second orgasm, when her body convulsed like something holy had left her.

Now, she leaned into him. Lucas washed her with slow and careful hands.

Over her shoulders, her back and between her thighs. When she flinched at the bruises, he kissed them.

When she hissed at the welt on her hip, he kissed that too.

She still didn't speak. Until he rinsed her hair and held her close again.

"I needed this," she whispered.

"I know."

"Not the pain."

"I know that too."

She looked up at him. "I needed to remember my body was mine. That I could give it, not as a wound but as a choice."

He nodded, his eyes burning.

"Thank you for taking it."

He kissed her hand. "Thank you for trusting me."

They sat in the water until it went cold.

Their breaths in sync with each other.

Then Amelia whispered, "After this is done….will you still want me?"

Lucas looked down and met her eyes.

"There isn't a version of you I don't want."

She blinked hard. "Even the one who kills?"

He smiled softly.

"Especially that one."

She buried her face in his chest and he held her like she'd just chosen to live again.

Chapter 37

The forest didn't breathe, not tonight.

Lucas moved like a ghost through the trees, low to the ground. His steps silent. Beside him, Amelia stalked with precision. No longer the girl who flinched at broken twigs or shadows that looked too much like him.

She was the thing men feared in their sleep. They'd left the estate an hour before sunset, dressed in black, the terrain mapped in their heads.

Every route, every fallback, every escape.

They weren't looking for Ethan. They were hunting his disciples.

The ones who delivered his messages. The ones who watched the house. The ones who still believed he was a God.

Amelia crouched behind a fallen log and raised the binoculars.

Three of them.

One was tall, twitchy and chewing gum like it was the only thing keeping his nerves in check.

The second was shorter with broad shoulders. Carried himself like someone who'd served time.

The third lingered in the back, pacing.

They weren't amateurs. But they weren't careful either.

Lucas knelt beside her, glancing at the men and then at her.

Her expression was made of stone. "They're waiting for something." she whispered.

Lucas nodded. "A signal maybe or a drop."

"Or him."

Lucas pulled a small tablet from his vest and tapped it twice.

Thermal imaging lit the screen. Four figures.

Amelia froze. "There's another."

"North ridge," Lucas said. "Higher ground, watching them."

"Not Ethan?"

"No" he zoomed in. "Wrong build."

"Still one of his," she whispered. "They don't move unless he tells them."

Silence stretched between them. Then Amelia stood.

Lucas grabbed her wrist. "Wait."

"I'm not going in." She pointed to the pacing man, the one in the back.

"He keeps checking his pocket."

Lucas followed her gaze. "Phone?"

"No, something else. It's like he is waiting to hand something off."

"Could be intel." Lucas's mouth tightened. "We follow them back."

She nodded and they moved, going parallel to the clearing.

Every step measured. The men below didn't know they were being watched but they soon would.

An hour passed, then two. The men broke formation and started walking. No words were exchanged, just a shift in body language.

Direction: East.

Away from the estate. Toward the back roads.

Amelia and Lucas trailed them from the ridge line, low and invisible.

Then the smallest one split off and took a side path, alone.

Amelia's pulse kicked and Lucas tilted his head at her like he was asking a question.

She nodded and he went after the remaining two, while she followed the stray.

The trees closed in tighter here. There was no moonlight or cover.

She stepped off the trail, her boots silent on the ground. Her knife rested in her belt and her gun was fully loaded. But she didn't reach for it. Not yet.

The man stopped near an old trail marker and looked around. Then pulled out a folded piece of paper. Set it down beneath a rock, turned and froze.

Amelia stepped from the trees like a ghost stitched from fog.

She didn't speak.

He went for his weapon she lunged forward and dropped him with one hit.

Boot to the back of the knee and elbow to the throat.

He hit the ground choking.

She knelt beside him and took his gun from his belt, pressing it to his cheek.

"I want you to tell him something," she whispered.

He wheezed. "Wh…who .."

She leaned closer. "I'm not hiding anymore."

Then Lucas was behind her. "Other two are heading toward a car. I got plates."

Amelia rose and tossed the gun into the bushes.

"He left a message," she said. "Same place as before."

Lucas's jaw clenched. "We pick him off next time."

She nodded once. "We take one alive."

Lucas looked at the man on the ground. "Starting now?"

Her smile was all teeth. "Yes."

She looked down at the man still coughing on the dirt. "This one will tell us everything he knows."

Thirty-Eight

Chapter 38

The man they dragged in was breathing too hard. He smelled like Ethan. Like fear wrapped in fake confidence. Lucas watched from the corridor as his men restrained him to the chair.

The man's lip was bleeding and his nose too. But the arrogance? That was still intact.

"You don't know who I am," the man spat. "You think this is going to scare me?"

Lucas didn't flinch. He just stepped into the room slowly, arms crossed and eyes cold.

"I know exactly who you are."

He dropped a folder onto the metal table beside the chair.

Inside: satellite captures, vehicle tags and digital timestamps. **Receipts.**

The man looked at them and smirked.

"You don't want me. You want him. I'm just logistics."

Lucas's expression didn't shift. "You're the rope in his hands."

The man sneered. "You think I knew what he was going to her? To any of them?"

"You knew enough to stay silent."

"I stayed alive."

Lucas leaned in, slow and deliberate, so close the man could feel the heat of his breath. His voice dropped to a whisper. "I can take that from you."

The smirk faltered, just slightly.

Lucas straightened, gave a single nod to Mason. "Leave us."

The team filed out, boots heavy against the concrete. The door clicked shut behind them.

The silence stretched, thick and expectant. Then she appeared.

Amelia stepped inside with the kind of quiet that made the air itself tense. The man blinked, startled. He hadn't noticed her behind Lucas.

She didn't look like the girl in the court photos, or the woman on the surveillance tapes.

She looked like the eye of the storm and when she spoke? It was quiet and even.

"He gave you orders. You followed them, now you will answer to me."

The man scoffed. "And who the fuck are you?"

Amelia stepped closer, hands behind her back. Still calm.

"I'm the reason you're bleeding."

He blinked again.

She turned to Lucas. "I want them room."

Lucas hesitated. "Are you sure?"

She nodded just once and then said. "You've done your part,

Lucas. Now let me do mine."

He didn't argue, he just turned and walked out the door, closing it behind him.

And for the first time, Amelia was alone with a man she didn't have to survive. She just had to break him.

The man sat chained to the chair, his breathing harder now.

He watched Amelia move like a shadow, slow and quiet.

She didn't ask if he was comfortable, didn't touch him, instead she pulled out the other chair and turned it backward. Straddled it like she was settling for a long night.

Then she placed a small box on the table and opened it.

Inside was a blade, a syringe, some zip ties and a recorder.

The man's eyes flickered to the contents and then back to her.

Still posturing.

Still trying to remember if she was the same woman who once cried in a courtroom, legs shaking and mascara streaked down her cheeks."

But this Amelia?

She didn't blink, she reached into the box and pulled out the recorder and clicked it on.

"State your name."

He laughed. "I want a lawyer."

"I want a time machine," she said softly. "One of us is going to get what we want tonight. Can you guess who?"

That made him straighten up.

"Now, let's try this again," she said. "Your name."

"Go to hell."

She smiled. "I've been there."

Amelia then stood up and walked behind him. Letting the silence crawl into his spine. When she spoke again, her voice was so close he could feel her breath at his ear.

"You think you're the first man to hold something over me?"

Her hand touched his shoulder. "You're just the last one who's going to survive it."

He snarled. "You're not going to do shit."

She gripped his jaw suddenly forcing his head back. "You're not the one who gets to make predictions anymore."

The first cut was shallow. Deliberate. Across the side of his thigh, where it would burn but not bleed too much.

He shouted.

She stepped and waited for a moment. "Ready to talk?"

"Fuck you, you bitch."

Amelia's head tilted slightly, like she was studying an insect pinned to glass. For a moment there was no sound but his ragged breathing.

She moved to the recorder and clicked it off. "No more witnesses."

What followed wasn't theatrical, it was systematic.

Amelia worked with measured precision. Spacing the pain between questions and watching his eyes, the way Lucas had once watched hers. Tracking dilation, breath and sweat.

"I used to think pain was something men gave to women like a curse."

A second cut, this time slightly deeper near the ribs. He jerked in the chair, a strangled cry ripping from his throat. His hands strained against the restraints and veins standing out on his arms.

"Fuck!" His voice cracked, somewhere between fury and fear. "You're insane!"

Amelia didn't blink. Her voice stayed steady, almost tender.

"No. Just fluent." She poured alcohol over the wound making him scream so loud she thought he might pass out.

"Do you know what he said the first time he hit me?" She asked calmly.

The man didn't answer.

"I made him feel powerless," she said. "So he made me feel small."

She brought the blade up to his forearm now and cut a single line, slow and clinical.

"I'm not small anymore."

He cracked after the fourth cut.

"Safe house… west side.. old boarding school… it's buried… no address… he moves the victims through tunnels…"

She went still. There were more victims? More then just her and Sophia?

"How many?" She whispered.

"I don't know…. three.. maybe more."

"Names!"

"I don't have them….I just helped move supplies and cash."

She stepped back.

"Who planted the second camera?" She asked. "There's someone else, in the house, still feeding him information and giving him access."

The man shook his head so fast the chair rattled.

"I don't…."

She didn't move, didn't even blink.

"Who!"

"I swear I don't know."

The blow came sudden. In one clean motion. It was the back of the blade's handle. His head snapped sideways with a crack;

blood sprayed across the floor.

For a moment he just sat there, stunned. Then the sound came. A low broken half sob, half curse.

Amelia didn't give him time to finish it. She stood over him like a verdict waiting to be spoken.

"He made me think submission meant weakness," she whispered. "You're going to die with a new definition in your head."

He sobbed. "I told you what I know."

Amelia stared at him, long and slow. Then leaned in and whispered in his ear, "Then you're no longer useful."

She opened the door, Lucas stood to the side and he looked back at her.

"Kill him," she said walking away.

Lucas didn't argue, he stepped inside and closed the door behind him.

The scream was short and final.

Amelia walked down the hall with blood still on her hands. She didn't wipe them, not yet. Because some stains weren't meant to be cleaned off.

They were meant to remind you who you've become.

Thirty-Nine

Chapter 39

Amelia sat on the edge of the bed, the letter paper before her untouched. The pen in her hand felt heavier then it should have.

It had written so many things, her statement to the court, the note to Ethan, her plan. But this?

This was the one thing she didn't want to put into words. Because this letter would only be opened if she was gone.

She took a breath and began writing:

To Lucas,

I didn't believe in redemption until I met you. Not the soft kind. Not the kind of people write poems about. I believed in survival, in keeping your head down, your hands clean and your screams locked in your ribs. But you never asked me to be soft.

You never told me to forget. You looked me in the eye when I was bloody and broken and said 'I'll stand behind you when you're ready to burn it down.'

You never flinched when I gave you the worst of me. You just knelt at my feet and handed me the knife.

You never saved me. You let me become something that didn't need saving.

And if you're reading this... I didn't make it.

But don't carry it.

Don't break open again for me. Don't lose the fire I lit in you.

You made me feel safe. But more then that, you made me dangerous again.

I loved you. I still do.

If I die, it won't be because I was weak.

It will be because I chose to walk into the fire, knowing I was a matchstick.

And knowing you'd still kiss me with ash on my skin.

xoxo Amelia

She folded the letter slowly. Her hands shook, but she didn't let them stop. She sealed it in a black envelope and a red wax stamp pressed into the flap.

Lucas's insignia. The only mark she trusted.

Downstairs, Lucas sat alone in the study.

He'd laid out the tools of war: Blueprints. Ammo. Surveillance prints.

But in front of him was only a blank page.

The same pen he used to write kill orders.

But this?

This wasn't about power, this was about truth.

He wrote in silence:

To Amelia,

You scare me. Not because you're violent. Not because you're unpredictable. But because you saw every inch of my darkness and decided you could love me anyway.

I wanted to protect you. But you didn't need protection. You needed someone to kneel when you couldn't stand.

Someone to kiss the edge of your blade and not look away.

You made me question everything I thought made me strong. And then you rebuilt me, quietly while bleeding.

If you're reading this, it means I died trying to keep you alive. And I'm okay with that.

Because you are the reason I didn't die all those years ago in that fucking house, with my mother drunk and my ribs cracked with nothing but rage left in me.

You made me something human again. So if you live, burn this letter. Forget me.

Not because I didn't matter but because you matter more.

Survive, Monroe.

And don't look back.

Lots of love
  Lucas.

He folded it and pressed a wax seal to the envelope.

Then carried it upstairs, where he found her standing on the balcony in the rain.

The storm had started without thunder. Just a slow fall of water that clung to her skin and made her look like something untouchable.

She turned when she heard him. She held out her letter and he did the same.

Neither of them spoke, they just exchanged them silently.

Then she stepped closer and kissed him, like she was tasting him for the last time.

"Are you ready?" she whispered.

"No," he said. "But I'm coming with you anyway."

"Don't die for me Lucas."

"Then live for me, Amelia."

They made love slow that night. No games, no sir, no pain. Just lips on scars and hands on hearts. Fingertips against ribs like they were counting the pieces left unbroken. And when they came together it wasn't with screams, it was with silence.

The kind that felt like a prayer. They fell asleep holding each other.

And when the first breach alert went off an hour before dawn… neither of them were surprised.

Forty

Chapter 40

The first alarm went off at 4:17 am.

Not a false trip. It was the fail-safe, the sensor that only activated if every outer line had already been breached.

Lucas's eyes flew open the second the tone hit.

Amelia was already moving, slipping from bed with a gun in one hand and her other grabbing the emergency phone off the dresser.

Lucas pressed a finger to his earpiece. "Talk."

Static.

Then Mason's voice, panicked and cut off.

"They're already inside….. north… flank… ambush!"

Then silence.

Amelia was out of the bedroom and down the hall before Lucas could speak.

She wasn't waiting. This was war.

By the time they hit the first floor, two of Lucas's men were already dead. Their bodies were twisted at the base of the staircase. One throat slit, the other shot through the temple.

No signs of forced entry.

No loud gunfire.

Silent kills.

Lucas swore under his breath.

"They had a way in," Amelia said coldly.

Lucas looked at her, eyes narrowed. "The mole."

They moved through the estate like they were made for it.

Tactical and precise.

Lucas handed her a second weapon. She took it, no questions.

Then the first shot rang out loud from the west hallway.

A spray of shattered glass followed.

They dropped instantly, their backs to the wall. Amelia peeked around the corner…..

Three men, maybe more. All wearing black masks and all carrying suppressed weapons. Military trained.

These were hired killers and at their centre was a figure not firing, not shouting just watching.

Tall and smiling beneath the shadows.

Ethan.

"Run," Lucas growled.

"No."

He turned to her eyes wild. "You're not dying here, Amelia."

"And you're not facing him alone."

Another explosion, this time closer.

The ceiling buckled.

Lucas grabbed her, pushed her through the back stairwell as debris rained down.

"Go to the panic hall. I'll follow. I just have to…"

"No!" she shouted. "We stay together!"

But it was too late. He shoved her hard through the last door, just as the floor above them collapsed. The impact was instant.

She screamed his name. "LUCAS!"

No response.

Smoke began pouring into the corridor. Her head rang and her knees buckled. But she crawled, screaming his name again. Then something slammed into the back of her skull and everything went black.

She woke to cold concrete against her cheek and her wrists throbbed, so did her temples.

She was on the floor, her hands tied behind her back. Ankles bound and her mouth was so dry.

It was too quiet. There were no alarms, no sirens and no Lucas.

Just the echo of her own breath.

Amelia blinked slowly, trying to focus.

The room was dim, there were no windows just a single hanging bulb above her, swaying like it had just been bumped.

The floor was damp and the air smelled like rot and bleach.

Behind her, a voice familiar. "You came back to me after all."

She didn't turn, didn't cry. She just said: "You're late."

Ethan laughed. Like this was a game they both remembered how to play.

"You used to be quieter when you were afraid."

"I used to be afraid of the wrong things."

"And now?"

"I'm only afraid of how slowly, I'm going to kill you."

A hand touched her shoulder. She didn't flinch. He walked around her to face her. Crouching low and peering into her eyes.

"You've gotten harder," he murmured.

"You've gotten desperate."

He leaned closer.

"I missed your mouth."

"I missed watching you bleed."

That made him smile but it didn't reach his eyes. They were hollow.

"I watched you, you know," he said. "Every night, with him. In his house. You on your knees moaning like a good little whore"

Amelia didn't blink, her silence was louder then a scream and he hated that.

"You watched me choose him. You watched me beg for what I wanted. Not like when I begged you to stop."

That wiped the smile clean off his face. He raised his hand and slapped her across the face. A fast, open-handed strike that snapped her head sideways. Her lip split, blood blooming across her tongue. She laughed.

The sound wasn't soft. It was a sound that didn't belong in a captive's throat. It belonged in a graveyard.

His hand clamped her jaw, squeezing until bone ground against bone.

"Still got that smart mouth."

She licked the blood from her teeth and grinned.

"Still got that soft dick?"

He hit her again, harder this time. Stars burst across her vision. Her cheek throbbed and her ears were ringing.

And still she smiled through it. To calm, to steady. "Is this how you get off now?" she rasped.

"On your knees, watching the playback of a woman who doesn't love you?"

Ethan stood and circled her. "You know," he said. "There was a time when you used to shake for me."

"There was a time I thought love meant pain. You trained me for that. Now I'm going to retrain myself with your corpse."

He yanked her to her knees by the hair. Jerking her head back so sharply her vision blurred. Her arms strained against the restraints until her skin burned, but she didn't make a sound.

"Say 'Sir,'" he hissed into her ear. "Beg me."

She leaned her head back, like a queen refusing to bow. Blood dripped from her chin.

"You first."

The snarl ripped out of him, guttural and animal like. He threw back to the ground. "I could fuck you until you break."

"You already did," she said calmly. Her voice was soft. That made it worse. "But I like the pieces better."

He began to pace, boots echoing in the hollow room. She watched as he started to unravel. She could feel it, his rage trying to find its way inside her. But she gave him nothing. No whimper. No pleading.

Her silence was like a blade. Her steadiness, a noose tightening around his ego.

He wanted terror but all he got was steel.

"Go ahead," she said. "Show me your masterpiece. Whatever you planned. Whatever footage you save. Make me watch."

"I don't need to make you watch."

"You need me afraid."

"I need you mine."

"You were never man enough to own me."

He lunged and grabbed her by the throat. Dragging her to the nearest wall and pinned her there.

One hand wrapped around her neck, the other yanked a knife from his belt and pressed it to her stomach.

"Then maybe I cut out the part of you that lies."

Her voice was a whisper, "You should've killed me when you had the chance."

He hesitated.

And that was his mistake.

Her head cracked forward, hard. Smashing into his nose. He screamed and dropped the knife.

She fell with him, landing on her knees and rolled kicking up with both bound legs, straight into his ribs.

He dropped, and she scrambled for the knife and sliced through the restraints. By the time he lunged again, she was on her feet, arm slashing out, the blade going across his forearm.

He screamed again.

"You thought I was the one on my knees," she said. "You forgot. I stood up."

He rushed her like a man possessed. They slammed into the wall hard. Breath ripped from her lungs as her back hit first. Her vision swam but she didn't fall. Ethan's body pinned her. Heavy and too close. She could feel his breath against her face. His other hand back around her throat.

He drove her up the wall, her feet barely touching the ground. Her windpipe compressed between his fingers.

"You think this makes you strong?" he hissed. "You're still

the same little bitch who cried when I looked at her too long."

Amelia's hands clawed at his wrists. Nails digging into flesh but he held tight.

Her vision dimmed and blood roared in her ears.

His free hand grabbed a fistful of her hair and yanked her head back, exposing her throat even more.

"I could squeeze until your eyes pop." He growled. "Make it slow. Make it biblical."

Her legs kicked, but she couldn't get leverage.

He shoved harder. Her lips parted on a choking gasp.

But she wasn't afraid. She was waiting.

His chest pressed flush against hers, weight keeping her trapped.

His rage was full now, his mask slipping.

"You don't get to win," he spat. "You don't get to walk away from me!"

Amelia's hand dropped to her hip, where the shard of broken glass she'd snatched during the fall was clutched tight in her palm.

She tightened her grip and she locked eyes with him. Then she smiled and drove the jagged edge up and deep into his lower abdomen. Right beneath his ribs.

Blood exploded against her hands, hot, thick and wet.

His mouth opened in a soundless scream. His whole body spasmed. His grip faltering. But she wasn't done. She twisted it, once and then twice.

Then yanked the shard out.

Ethan fell backward with a sound that wasn't human. He crumpled. Hands to his gut, blood pouring between his fingers,

He coughed and choked. But Amelia wasn't watching anymore. She dropped the glass and collapsed to her knees gasping for air. Her hand on her throat and the other braced against the wall.

She didn't speak, didn't cry, just watched him writhe. Not dead yet, but dying.

"Feel that?" she rasped. "That's what survival tastes like."

He whimpered and tried to reach for her ankle, she kicked his hand away and sat there, bruised, bleeding but alive.

Until everything went dark.

Chapter 41

Her hands were wrapped in gauze, tight and stinging, the way they used to be after she bled them trying to claw her way out of Ethan's old apartment.

Except this wasn't the past. This was after.

Her eyes opened slowly. Dim lights above her, the soft hum of medical monitors and the smell of antiseptic filled her.

She wasn't in that concrete room anymore. She wasn't alone. "Hey."

The voice cut through the haze like a blade wrapped in velvet. Lucas.

She turned her head toward the sound and winced. A bolt of fire shooting through her neck.

He was seated in a chair beside her bed, one arm in a sling, dried blood still flaking along his jawline. His left eye was swollen and his lip split.

But he was alive and so was she.

"You shouldn't be sitting up," his voice low. "You've been through hell."

Her voice was gravel. "I stabbed him."

Lucas nodded once. "There was so much blood, Amelia. When we found you…"

"Where is he?" She interrupted.

Lucas hesitated. She knew before he even spoke.

"Gone."

She tried to sit up more but her body screamed. Lucas was beside her in an instant, hands catching her shoulders, gently guiding her back.

"They found you in the sub-level under the greenhouse. You were unconscious. He was…gone."

Her throat tightened.

"No."

"There was blood everywhere, a lot and the shard…" he swallowed. "was still in your hand."

"But his body wasn't there?"

"Vanished, no drag marks, no trail." He held her gaze. And she saw it there, the guilt. The same helpless guilt she'd worn after Sophia.

"He didn't die," she whispered.

Lucas didn't answer. He didn't need to. She turned her head toward the window.

"I felt it," she said. "The glass went in, he bled on me."

Lucas reached for her hand and took it gently between his hands.

"You saved your own life."

"No," her voice cracked. "I was supposed to end his."

Lucas stroked his thumb along her knuckles. His skin rough

and still bruised.

"I need to see it."

"You're not ready to walk," he murmured. "Give it a few more hours."

"No, I need to see the room where I left him now!."

Lucas hesitated but then nodded.

"I'll take you but only when you're steady. I promise."

"Thank you," she said quietly.

He didn't respond right away, then softly, "I hate that I couldn't get to you first."

She turned her head toward him.

"You found me."

"Not before he put his hands on you."

She reached for him, gently this time. "I fought back," she whispered. "He had his hand on my throat and I still took him down."

Lucas exhaled. A rough shaking breath. "I know and I've never been more fucking in love with you."

* * *

They descended into the sub-level just after midnight. Lucas had tried to talk her out of it, said she needed more time to heal. But she had to see it for herself. Healing came later, this? This was confirmation.

She walked slowly, every joint aching. But her spine was straight.

Lucas stayed at her side, flashlight cutting narrow beams through the dark.

The hallway smelled like rot and iron. The scent of blood

that hadn't been cleaned.

It led them straight to the door. The one she remembered, as she fought Ethan with a shard of broken glass in her hand.

Lucas unlocked it, the bolt screeching as the door opened.

And the moment the light cut through, Amelia stopped breathing.

Blood, so much blood. All dried now. Streaked across the floor in a pattern only someone like her would recognise.

There were no drag marks, no footprints, no signs of forced entry from the outside.

Just blood and air.

Amelia stepped inside, she looked down and saw her own hand print pressed in blood. Where she'd braced herself during the final blow. She knelt beside it to remember.

"He didn't die here." She whispered.

Lucas didn't move. "He should have."

Amelia nodded slowly. "Then someone helped him."

She stood slowly, and walked the perimeter of the room. There was a shelf against the far wall. Old and rusty. Mostly empty but there was something in the centre of it.

She approached it slowly. Her blood ran cold.

A camera.

And beside it the mirror shard. Angled deliberately upward, so that when she reached for the camera… She saw her own reflection.

Etched into the back of the glass, faint but unmistakable:
Soon.

She didn't scream, she didn't drop it. She turned slowly and showed it to Lucas .

"He left it for you." He said.

"No," she whispered. "He left it for both of us."

Lucas walked to her and took the mirror gently from her hand. Then without a word he crushed it in his palm. Blood ran down his wrist.

"He thinks he still has time."

Amelia looked back at the pool of dried blood where Ethan should have died.

Then at the empty floor, and then the crushed mirror.

"Then we make time his enemy."

Forty-Two

Chapter 42

The sky was a dull grey canvas as dawn began to break.

What was left of the estate groaned under the weight of silence.

Charred beams exposed. Smoke-stained glass littered the floors.

The scent of ash and metal still clung to the walls.

The ceiling above the main hall had caved in, letting the pale morning light pour through in jagged slants.

Amelia stood amongst the wreckage, wrapped in a blanket.

Lucas moved carefully, his limp barely visible. One hand braced on the door frame for balance.

"I remember thinking this place would always be safe," she said. Her voice hollow.

Lucas came to stand beside her. "Was it ever?"

She looked at him, then at the ruin behind him. "Maybe not. But I needed to believe it."

Lucas reached down and picked up a shard of glass from the floor. He held it between two fingers and then tossed it aside.

It landed without a sound in the ash.

They walked in silence through the rest of the wreckage.

She touched the edge of a scorched doorway.

"Do you think he planned this?" she asked.

Lucas nodded. "Yep, every single second of it."

"I mean the ending. Letting me think I'd won."

Lucas looked at her. At the cuts down her arms, the burst vessels in her eyes. The way she didn't flinch at the brokenness anymore.

"No," he said. "I think he wanted to kill you and you reminded him what it feels like to bleed."

They stopped at the edge of the greenhouse, the only place still partially intact.

Amelia stepped into it. Debris gave way beneath her feet.

Lucas didn't follow her in right away. He watched her instead. Watched the way she picked up a crushed flowerpot. The way she set it upright again, even if nothing was left inside.

"It's not over," she said.

Lucas moved beside her.

"No. But this battle is."

She turned, her face raw and exhausted.

"He's still out there."

Lucas pulled something from his jacket. A blade. Compact and sharp. He placed it in her hand.

"Then next time, make it count."

She gripped the hilt, tight. "I want to be the one who ends him," she whispered.

Lucas reached for her and held the side of her face in his calloused palm.

"And I'll be the one who helps you bury him."

About the Author

Chantel Nunn writes stories for the women who've been through hell and still crave love that consumes them. Her words live in the shadows , exploring trauma, trust, obsession, and the kind of dark romance that doesn't ask you to be perfect… just *honest.*

A bookish witch at heart, Chantel blends emotional healing, sensual surrender, and power reclamation into every page she writes. Her heroines are soft but not fragile. Her men? Dangerous, devoted, and just unhinged enough to ruin your standards.

When she's not writing fictional chaos, you'll find her lighting candles, pulling tarot cards, baking in her kitchen like a cozy domestic goddess, or creating bookish magic for her small business. She believes love should feel like safety and fire , and her stories make space for both.